UPSIDE★DOWN MAGIC

UPSIDE ★ DOWN MAGIC

by

Sarah
MLYNOWSKI,

Lauren
MYRACLE,

and

Emily
JENKINS

Scholastic Press/New York

Library of Congress Cataloging-in-Publication Data available

ISBN 978-0-545-80045-7

10 9 8 7 6 5 4 3 2   16 17 18 19

Printed in the U.S.A.   23
First edition, October 2015

Book design by Abby Dening

For David, of course.

Nory Horace was trying to turn herself into a kitten.

The kitten had to be a black kitten. And it had to be completely kitten-shaped.

It was the middle of summer. Nory was hiding in her family's garage. *Kitten, kitten, kitten,* she thought.

She was hiding in case something went wrong. She didn't want anyone to see. Still, if something went *really* wrong, her brother and sister would be close enough to hear her yell for help.

Or meow for help.

Or roar.

Nory decided not to think about that. Hopefully, she wouldn't need help.

Kitten, kitten, kitten.

She had to master kitten, because tomorrow was the Big Test. Tomorrow, after so many years of waiting, she would finally take the entrance exam for Sage Academy.

The school was very hard to get into. You wouldn't be accepted with anything less than amazing talents. Nory's friends weren't even bothering to try. They were all taking tests for easier schools.

If Nory passed the Big Test, she would start fifth grade at Sage Academy in the fall.

If she failed the test . . .

No. She couldn't fail. She wasn't taking tests for any other schools. Not only because Sage Academy was a very important, very fancy magic school, but also because her brother, Hawthorn, went there.

And her sister, Dalia, did, too.

Plus, Nory's father was kind of the headmaster.

Okay, not kind of. He was definitely the headmaster.

Thinking about the Big Test made Nory queasy. Her magic was strong. There was no doubt about that. But sometimes her magic went wonky.

And Sage Academy did not want wonky.

A black kitten was likely to be on the Big Test tomorrow. It was a beginner animal. Nory had turned herself into a black kitten loads of times, actually. The problem was what happened *after.*

But Nory would not think about that. Instead, she took a deep breath and lifted her chin.

Kitten! Kitten! KITTEN!!!

The world went blurry, and Nory's heart beat faster. Her body stretched and shrank. There were popping sounds.

Yay, kitten!

But wait.

Her mouth felt wrong. Nory clacked her teeth together. Clack, clack, clack. *Whoa.*

These weren't normal teeth. These were long. These were sharp. These were powerful. Long, sharp, and powerful enough to chomp through wood!

Hmm, Nory thought, feeling odd. *Why would a kitten want to chomp wood?*

Nory looked over her shoulder. She saw a perfect black kitten tail swishing in the air. Connected to the tail was a set of black kitten legs, with padded feet and sharp claws.

She looked down, expecting to see a matching set of front legs where her arms used to be. But . . .

Her front legs weren't kitten legs. The fur was brown and slick. Also, she seemed to have a fat, round tummy. And what was this nose?

She couldn't see it well, but it had nothing kitten-ish about it. It was more of a snout.

A beaver nose.

Zamboozle! I'm half kitten and half beaver, Nory realized.

Her magic.

Had definitely.

Gone wonky.

Not again! she thought. *What am I doing wrong? I'll fail the Big Test if I do this tomorrow! I should change back right away and try again for perfect kitten. Yes. That's exactly what I should do.*

But the beaver-kitten part of Nory wouldn't listen. Beaver-Kitten-Nory didn't care about the Big Test. Beaver-Kitten-Nory just wanted to chew stuff with her awesome beaver teeth.

She searched the garage. Wood! Where was the wood around here?

Must chew, Beaver-Kitten-Nory thought. *Must make beaver dam.*

No! No! said the dim voice of Girl-Nory.

Beaver-Kitten-Nory waddled out of the garage and into the house. Then she went upstairs and into her father's office. Tree stumps would do, or branches. Anything, really, made of wood.

Nory spotted her father's bookshelf.

It was very beautiful, having been lovingly built over two hundred years ago by craftsmen in Europe.

It was a very important, very expensive piece of furniture.

It looked delicious.

Oooh, Beaver-Kitten-Nory thought. *Look at that! A wooden tall-thing! Chewy rectangle-things!*

She nudged one of the books onto the floor and nibbled it.

Hard on the outside, like bark. Tender on the inside, like leaves. *Mmm. Chew, chew, chew.* Beaver-Kitten-Nory gnawed through four of her father's books.

Then she bit through the legs of her father's solid oak desk.

Next she chewed off a section of her father's favorite armchair. She dragged fluff and wood into the guest bathroom and built a small beaver lodge under the sink. Then she chased her kitten tail for a couple minutes and used a pile of ripped-up pages for a litter box.

It was awesome. *She* was awesome. She, Beaver-Kitten-Nory, felt better than she had in weeks!

At least, until her brother, Hawthorn, found her.

2

Hawthorn was sixteen. He took care of most of the house stuff because their father, Dr. Horace, was too busy and important to be bothered with making dinner and braiding hair.

And because their mother wasn't around.

She had died a long time ago.

Hawthorn liked sports and cooking and bossing people around. He also liked setting things on fire, since he was a Flare. A really good Flare, too. His powers never went wonky.

"Nory!" Hawthorn cried now, staring at the beaver lodge. "What are you doing?"

Beaver-Kitten-Nory tried to rub her face on Hawthorn's pant leg.

"I don't even know what you are right now," he went on, "but you better change back and help me clean up. Seriously, what have you done? It stinks in here!"

His voice made Beaver-Kitten-Nory tremble.

"Nory? Change back *now*!" Hawthorn yelled.

Ploof. He'd scared Nory into returning to her proper girl shape: big hair, small body, brown skin, purple shirt. There was a bit of armchair fabric stuck in her teeth. Yuck. She spit it out.

This was a disaster.

The office and the bathroom were smelly messes. Father's favorite armchair looked like it had exploded. His antique desk tilted dangerously on three legs. Some of his precious books now resembled coleslaw.

He was going to be really, *really* angry.

"Sorry," Nory whispered.

Hawthorn looked mad. And scared.

"Just help me clean," he told his sister. "We don't have long."

Together they fixed up the damage as well as they could. They filled garbage bag after garbage bag. They wiped surfaces with spray cleaner. When the bathroom looked like a bathroom again, Hawthorn called a carpenter to repair the desk and armchair. He made Nory vacuum up the wood dust. He found the website for the Cup and Chaucer Bookshop and ordered new copies of all the books Nory had ruined.

When all this was done, Nory cleared her throat and asked, "Hawthorn? Are you still mad at me?"

He shook his head. "You have to keep your human mind in control, Nory. That's all there is to it."

"I know."

"And when you turn into an animal, turn into a *normal* animal," he snapped. "Stop mixing your parts up. You're getting really wonky and nobody likes it."

"I was practicing kitten like you told me to," Nory explained. "And then the beaver part just happened, and everything went upside down."

"That's what you were?" asked Hawthorn. "A kitten-beaver?"

"Beaver-kitten, actually," said Nory. She thought for a moment, then grinned. "A bitten!"

"Whatever it was, it was gross," Hawthorn said.

Nory's grin disappeared.

"Plus, you lost control, like you always do," Hawthorn continued. "We'll have to blame Dalia's rabbits, I guess."

Dalia, the middle Horace child, was thirteen. She was a Fuzzy and had a lot of pets, including two bats, three toads, a ferret, a toucan, a pair of mice, and twelve rabbits. They weren't well behaved. The ferret pooped on the carpet. So did the toads. And the bats were always going in people's hair. It wasn't a stretch to blame Nory's mess on the bunnies.

Still, Nory felt guilty. The rabbits shouldn't get in trouble for her mistake. Neither should Dalia. She twisted her hands. "Shouldn't we tell Father what really happened?"

"No," Hawthorn said. "We don't want him angry at you. Not the day before the Big Test."

Nory bowed her head. Maybe Hawthorn was right. Some lies were safer than the truth.

Up until summer vacation, Nory had gone to ordinary school like everyone else her age. Nory's ordinary school was called Woody Dale. It was kindergarten through fourth grade, just like all other ordinary schools.

Nory had studied reading and writing, math and science, gym, art, and music. The one thing she hadn't studied was magic, since a person's powers didn't bubble up until around the time she or he turned ten. Once you were ten and ready for fifth grade, you enrolled in a different school. You still had to read and do math and play basketball, but you also practiced magic. The kind of magic you practiced depended on your talent.

Some kids were Flares—they had fire talents, like Hawthorn.

Some were Fuzzies—they had animal talents, like Dalia.

Others were Flickers or Flyers or Fluxers. Nory was a Fluxer, although she wasn't a regular Fluxer.

Her magic was unusually big. Unlike most Fluxers, she could turn into lots of animals. But Nory hid her magic from Father, because it always went wonky.

For example, she'd be a perfectly nice skunk and suddenly swell up to the size of an elephant. And then grow a trunk.

Or she'd be a perfectly nice puppy and then grow squid legs.

Nory knew that Father would disapprove of a puppy with squid legs. He would disapprove *a lot*.

Another problem was that Girl-Nory almost always lost control of her human self during her transformations and ended up making a huge mess.

Skunkephant-Nory had become obsessed with finding peanuts and had stunk up the Horace kitchen. They'd had to scrub everything with bleach and convince Father that some real skunks had snuck through the kitchen window. Puppy-Squid-Nory had chewed all of Dalia's shoes and then squirted Hawthorn with nasty squid ink. Hawthorn had claimed he'd been the victim of an exploding pen.

Even black kitten had gone wrong four different ways. The scariest was when Nory had developed a touch of dragon and breathed fire at the sofa. Hawthorn had taken the blame for that one, telling Father he'd goofed up a Flare seat-warming project. Father had bought a new sofa and made Hawthorn pay for part of it, but Nory wondered if he'd really been fooled. Hawthorn got top marks in Flare Studies at Sage Academy. He never would have made a mistake like that.

Father must have known that Nory's transformation power was out of control.

He just didn't want to talk about it.

He didn't talk about a lot of things.

When Father got home from Sage Academy that evening, Hawthorn told him about the damage. Immediately, Father marched to his office to see it for himself. Hawthorn, Dalia, and Nory followed.

"Dalia," Father said, frowning at the scratch marks on his desk. "You have got to get those rabbits in line. Discipline is what they need. Discipline and a better lock on their pen. You'll take care of that, yes?"

"Yes, Father," Dalia said. She glared at Nory.

Father hesitated. "Well. Thank you, Hawthorn, for calling the carpenter and for ordering new copies of my books."

Hawthorn nodded. Father glanced at Nory. For a second, she thought he was going to say something to her.

Maybe he would ask her what really happened.

Maybe he'd offer his help.

Instead, he clenched and unclenched his fingers three times. The entire messed-up office disappeared around them.

Most Flickers could make things invisible, but only extremely powerful Flickers could make an entire room disappear while people were still standing in it. All the edges were neat and even, too. The Horace family appeared to be hovering above the dining room.

"Go downstairs, children," Father said. "I'd prefer not to be disturbed for the rest of the evening."

He himself disappeared, and the conversation was over.

Father left early for work the next morning.

Nory ate breakfast with Dalia, Hawthorn, and a few of Dalia's rabbits.

"Do you want your egg hard- or soft-boiled?" Hawthorn asked. He took a raw egg from the refrigerator.

"Soft, please," Nory answered.

Hawthorn cooked the egg the way all Flares did, heating it with his hands until it was perfectly done. Then he shot flames from his fingertips and toasted a piece of bread. As he served Nory her food, he said, "Eat up—you'll need your energy. Are you ready for the Big Test?"

Nory nodded. Then she shook her head. Then she nibbled at her toast.

"Just do what the teachers ask," Hawthorn advised. "Not more, not less. Don't get weird."

"I know," said Nory. She tried to swallow but the breadcrumbs stuck in her throat.

"They want you to be predictable."

"I know."

"And precise."

"I know."

"So get your details correct, down to the whiskers."

"Okay."

"Keep control of the animal body."

"Okay."

"And braid your hair. Tight! Also, you can't wear those pants."

Nory looked down at her clothes. "But these are my lucky purple jeans!"

Hawthorn shook his head. "Change into that dress with the nice collar."

Nory stood up.

"Not now! After breakfast!"

Nory sat down, and Hawthorn gave her more instructions. Dalia joined in, too. They talked at her while she tried to eat. They talked at her through the door while she changed her outfit. They talked at her all the way to Sage Academy, which was a ten-minute walk from their house.

They led her through the school gates and paused. Hawthorn placed his hands on Nory's shoulders. "Whatever happens, whatever you turn into, don't lick anything."

"Or eat anything," said Dalia.

Hawthorn hugged Nory. "Just do your best."

"And pass the test," Dalia added.

"Not that we're worried!" they said together.

Then they were gone. Hawthorn was expected at his summer job. Dalia had an appointment with her math tutor.

Nory was on her own.

The building that held Sage Academy's Hall of Magic and Performance was tall and made of stone. Gargoyles looked down from above.

Inside, Nory found a line of kids standing with their parents. They were all there for the Big Test.

Mothers smoothed their children's hair. Fathers patted shoulders and buttoned cardigans.

Nory's dress was itchy.

In front of her was a light-skinned girl with a sharp, short haircut. Her features were small, her hands were small, and her feet were small. The only big thing about her was her glasses. They had black frames. Each lens was the size of a large cookie.

The girl's dad spoke to her in a low voice. "You

can light matches, Lacey. We know that. But let's go over the marshmallow."

"Golden brown is four seconds, slightly burnt is six," the girl—Lacey—recited. Her lip trembled.

"If you undercook it, you won't get into Sage Academy," her dad warned. "If you overcook it, that's even worse."

Lacey nodded.

"Don't mess up," said the dad.

Lacey's hands started to shake.

Nory felt bad for her. She didn't think Lacey's dad was being particularly helpful. She tapped Lacey on the shoulder and smiled.

"This is scary, isn't it?" Nory said. "My stomach's like one huge knot."

Lacey whipped around. "Shhhh! Don't you realize people are concentrating? People are reviewing their magic techniques!"

Nory blushed. She chewed the inside of her cheeks and waited.

The line moved forward.

Now ten kids were in line ahead of her.

Then eight. Then five.

Then one. Lacey's name was called, and a look of pure panic flashed across her face.

"Good luck," Nory said.

"*Shhhh!*" Lacey said again. She smoothed out her expression, shrugged off a hug from her father, and marched into the Hall of Magic and Performance to take the Big Test.

Silence.

More silence.

Then, from behind the Hall of Magic and Performance door, great racking sobs.

Lacey burst out of the room, ran down the long hall, and pushed through the heavy doors of the building.

"Lacey?" the girl's dad cried, dashing after his daughter. "Lacey!"

Lacey's wails sounded ghostly.

Nory shivered.

It was her turn.

3

The Hall of Magic and Performance was very grand. The ceilings were painted with dragons and unicorns. The seats were covered in dark purple velvet. The curtains on the side of the stage were gold. A large chandelier hung from the ceiling, lit by candles.

Onstage was a wooden table that looked to be as old as the school itself. Nory walked onto the stage and faced the audience. Seated in the front row were four teachers and her father, the headmaster. He wore his second-best suit.

He didn't smile. He sat rigid.

He didn't have to tell anyone that Nory was his daughter. Everybody knew.

Nory's legs wobbled.

"State your name," commanded Mr. Puthoor. Nory had met him before, when she'd attended school events with her siblings. In all those times, she'd never seen him smile. Not once.

"Elinor Boxwood Horace," she answered. "But everybody calls me Nory."

Mr. Puthoor drew his eyebrows together. "We will begin with basic tests, Ms. Horace. If you show talent in one area of magic, we will ask to see more of what you can do in that category."

Nory nodded.

"For example," continued Mr. Puthoor, "the Flare test begins with lighting a match. If you can do that, we will ask you to roast a marshmallow, then cook an egg, and so forth."

Nory nodded again.

"However, if you cannot light the match, you are not a Flare, in which case we will move on to the next category. Do you understand?"

"Yes."

"Please approach the table, Ms. Horace."

Nory stepped forward. On the table was a box.

"You may open it," said Mr. Puthoor.

Nory opened it and pulled out a large warty toad. It croaked and blinked its bulging eyes.

"Make the toad disappear," Mr. Puthoor instructed.

This is the Flicker test, then, thought Nory. Making things turn invisible, like her father could.

Nory figured she might as well give it a shot. It would be so great to be a Flicker like her father and not a messed-up Fluxer.

She closed her eyes.

She tried to erase that toad with her mind.

She really, really tried.

No toad, no toad, no toad.

She opened her eyes.

The toad was still there. Its eyes were still bulging.

The teachers made marks in their notebooks. Nory's father pursed his lips and made the toad disappear himself.

Next, Mr. Puthoor stepped onto the stage and produced a box of matches. He set the box on the table, took out a single match, and held it out to Nory.

"Light this for us without striking it."

The Flare test. Flares could manipulate fire and heat, like Hawthorn did.

Maybe I can do this one! Nory thought. She had lit the sofa on fire, after all. That time she came down with a small case of dragon.

Don't even think about it! Or it might happen.

Nory shook her head. "I can't," she told Mr. Puthoor.

The teachers made marks in their notebooks.

"All right, then," said Mr. Puthoor. "Lift yourself into the air. Two feet from the floor, precisely."

Oh! Nory thought. *The Flyer test!*

Nory wasn't a Flyer, but she had indeed flown. More than once. For example, in January, she had turned into a mouse with bluebird wings and—

Nope, nope, nope. They do not want to see that.

These professors wanted normal Flyer flying.

Nory contracted her muscles. She sensed her face turning red.

Up up up up up up up up UP.

She remained firmly on the floor.

"Silly faces won't make you fly, Ms. Horace," Mr. Puthoor scolded. "Let's move on. I will summon Pokey."

He whistled a short melody. A silver unicorn peeked out from backstage. Shyly, it trotted out.

"As you know, unicorns do not like mushrooms," Mr. Puthoor said. "And they're quite skittish around most humans."

A small pile of mushrooms appeared on the table in front of Nory.

"Convince Pokey to nibble them from your hand."

The Fuzzy test, then. Animal magic. Dalia could do this in a heartbeat.

Nory scooped up the mushrooms. "Here, girl," she said. "Here, Pokey." She took a step toward the unicorn.

Pokey whinnied and stepped away.

"No, Pokey, you *like* mushrooms. Yummy yummy *mush*rooms!"

Pokey stepped back again.

"Enough," Mr. Puthoor said wearily, but Nory kept trying.

"Come on, Pokey. Be a big brave unicorn! I won't hurt you." She took a deep breath. "Eat the mushrooms! Pretty please?" Nory moved a step forward.

Pokey reared onto her hind legs and bolted. She galloped three times around the stage before leaping off and thundering down the aisle. She made a sharp right in the lobby and disappeared up the stairs.

Nory wanted to hide.

Four tests failed.

Pokey afraid. Mr. Puthoor exasperated. Her father, frozen in his seat.

Still, the Fluxer test would be next. She could do it. She knew she could.

4

Nory's father rose. "There is one category left," he said in a great, booming voice. It was the voice he used when addressing large crowds. Also, sometimes, at home. "Please turn yourself into a black kitten, Ms. Horace."

Nory concentrated. Hard.

Kitten, she thought. *Kitten, kitten, kitten!*

Like before, she felt her body shift, her vision blur. Popping noises. She concentrated on the details she knew the teachers would want to see: whiskers, claws, a bit of fluff in the ears. And . . .

Nory was a kitten! A black one, too, from what she could see of her paws.

"Very nice," said Mr. Puthoor.

Yes! Yes! Yes! Girl-Nory thought.

Kitten-Nory purred.

"Dr. Horace will now check the details," Mr. Puthoor said.

Nory's father climbed onstage. He looked down at Kitten-Nory. She jumped onto the table and licked her paw, showing off.

Father's eyes were serious behind his glasses, but Kitten-Nory thought he looked pleased. He bent over her.

Her senses went on high alert. What was that good smell?

Fish!

Fish! Fish! Fish!

Ignore that fish! Girl-Nory tried to tell Kitten-Nory. Father liked to eat smoked salmon for breakfast. There was a smell of it left on his hands, that was all.

But Kitten-Nory couldn't help it.

Fish!

No fish for you!

Father reached to pet her. His hand smelled yummy.

Fish! Fish! Fish!

Kitten-Nory's jaw unhinged like a snake's.

A snake? Was she a snake-kitten now? A snitten?

SNAP!

Nory chomped her father's hand with her snitten jaw.

He yelped in pain and tried to shake her off, but she held on.

Fish!

STOP IT NOW!

Fish!

That is not a salmon! That is Father!

Fish!

You will never get into Sage Academy if you eat the headmaster!

Fish!

STOP!

Fish!

YOUR ENTIRE FUTURE IS AT STAKE!!!

Oh, fine. With a wrench, Snitten-Nory let go of her father's hand.

Slowly, Nory felt the snake in her disappear.

Phew. Now she was just a kitten again. A good black kitten, she was pretty sure. So maybe she could pass this test after all? It had been only a minute of snitten. Maybe they hadn't even noticed.

Nory felt a tingling on her shoulders.

What was happening? She squirmed to look.

Oh, no.

She had sprouted wings. Enormous wings that were three times the size of her kitten body.

Huge claws burst out of her kitten paws.

Flap. Flap! Roar!

She leapt into the air. She swooped around the auditorium with her big dragon wings.

She was a full-on dragon-kitten now!

How awesome is this? Dritten-Nory thought. *So awesome!*

Girl-Nory disagreed. *No, not awesome! Just be a normal kitten!*

But Dritten-Nory wasn't going to listen.

No way. Flying is too much fun! Maybe it's time to breathe some fire, yeah?

No fire! thought Girl-Nory.

Yes fire! thought the Dritten. *And that unicorn— what a yummy snack a unicorn would be!*

Wait! thought Girl-Nory. *Stop. Calm down. Fly lower.*

Maybe she could still fix things. In fact, she had an idea. A good idea.

And if the idea worked, Nory might get into Sage Academy after all.

Dritten-Nory flew down from the high ceiling of the hall. As the teachers watched, she flapped her wings and hovered over the stage—two feet above the floor, precisely.

Just like the Flyer test.

Did the teachers notice?

Yes, they did! They were scribbling in their notebooks.

Then, because she might as well try, Dritten-Nory went for the Flare test. With a great puff, she set the entire box of matches on fire.

Wahoo! Fluxer, Flyer, and Flare—that was three out of five categories!

Would they consider her a triple talent?

Even if they didn't, it was going to be okay. She had big magic! That had to be worth something.

Or was she really, REALLY failing the Big Test?

Her sudden doubt knocked the excitement out of her. She turned back into a girl.

"Thank you very much for testing me," Nory said. She forced a smile just the way Hawthorn had told her to. She used her very best manners.

The teachers continued making marks in their notebooks. But Father couldn't. He was cradling his swelling hand. His swelling, bleeding hand.

The teachers looked stern. Finally they stopped

writing and put their heads together. They whispered fiercely.

Nory went cold.

Mr. Puthoor looked up. "Miss Horace, I'm sorry. We can't have such wonky magic here at Sage Academy. No matter how big your power, and no matter who your family is."

"But—"

"Your magic is damaged somehow."

Nory looked at her father.

Her father looked at her.

"Agreed," he said grimly. "Elinor Boxwood Horace, your admission is denied."

5

That evening, Father and Hawthorn picked at their dinner. Dalia ate only half a turnip. Nory couldn't even manage that. Her throat was clogged with held-back tears.

No one talked about what had happened. No one spoke at all.

As soon as he finished his food, Father turned invisible and went to his still-invisible office. He didn't come out for the rest of the night.

Hawthorn let Nory stay up late in front of the

television. He made her toasted marshmallows. Dalia coaxed a rabbit to cuddle in Nory's lap.

Still, they didn't talk about what happened. Not that night, nor any of the days and nights afterward.

Nory wasn't sure what happened to kids who didn't get into any schools.

Nobody would tell her. The one time she asked Hawthorn, he said not to worry about it now.

Lots of kids went to public schools, but Father didn't like them. He would hire a governess, maybe, to teach her at home.

Summer stretched toward fall. Nory played with her friends from Woody Dale Ordinary School. She heard them talk about the schools they'd gotten into. She admired their new talents without ever showing them hers.

She read books. She watched movies. She kicked a soccer ball around the yard. She remained scared to ask Father what would happen to her when school started, so she never did.

One cool August evening, Father's phone beeped during dinner. He checked it and pushed back his chair.

"She's on her way," he said to Hawthorn. "You'll take care of everything?"

Hawthorn hesitated. Then he dropped his gaze. "I will," he said.

Father strode from the room, going invisible as he did so.

"Who's on her way?" Nory asked. "What will you take care of?"

Hawthorn lit his paper napkin on fire and put it out again.

Dalia offered a spoonful of jam to the ferret at her feet.

"What's going on?" Nory persisted.

"I'm here!" called a vibrant voice from outside.

Through the open kitchen window flew a sturdy-looking white woman. She wore jeans and sneakers. Her short hair was sticking up every which way. She swerved neatly into the dining room and lowered herself gently onto the floor.

Nory's mouth fell open. It was Aunt Margo. She hadn't been to visit since Nory's mother had died six years before.

Margo hugged Hawthorn and Dalia, saving Nory for last. "Oh, my little Nory. You've grown so big!"

"I have?"

"And I hear you're *quite* a talent. Have you got your stuff?"

"Huh?"

Aunt Margo's eyebrows shot up. "Shirts, jeans, jammies. Your toothbrush. I can come back for your cold-weather clothes, but you'll need the basics."

Nory turned to Dalia and Hawthorn. They wouldn't meet her eyes.

"Oh, seriously!" said Aunt Margo. "Did they not tell you?"

"Tell me what?" Nory replied in a tiny voice.

"Sheesh. Why doesn't anyone in this family *talk* about anything?"

"Sorry," muttered Hawthorn. "I was getting around to it."

Aunt Margo lifted off the floor so high she nearly touched the dining room ceiling. She banged on it with her fist. "You need to talk about things, Stone!" she yelled to Nory's father. "It's bad to not talk about things with your own children!"

Nory gaped.

"He won't listen to me," Margo said, lowering herself back to the floor. "He never did and never will. But it still feels good to speak my mind."

Nory thought it would feel even better to change the subject. "Father said you drive a taxi," she blurted. "He says you don't get paid much. Actually, he says you're poor, which is why we haven't seen you in forever."

"Nory!" Dalia scolded.

"Meh," said Aunt Margo. "I'm not poor. I'm just not rich. And I don't drive a taxi. I *am* a taxi." She pointed to the logo on the front of her T-shirt: DOUBLE M FLYING TAXI.

Despite herself, Nory was impressed. All Flyers could fly, or they wouldn't be Flyers. But very few could take passengers.

Hawthorn went to the coat closet and pulled out a blue duffel bag. He put it by the front door. "I got her packed," he said, not looking at Nory.

Nory's lip trembled. "Father's getting rid of me? Because I flunked the Big Test?"

"It's not like that," said Dalia.

"It's just for a little while," Hawthorn promised.

"For your education," said Dalia. "You'll come visit on holidays. It'll be fun!"

"He's ashamed of me," said Nory. Her eyes teared up. "You're all ashamed of me!"

Aunt Margo shook her head. "Not true. They want what's best for you. And I can't wait to get to know you again."

The energy drained from Nory's body.

Father. Hawthorn. Dalia. The two bats, the three toads, the ferret, the toucan, the pair of mice, and the twelve rabbits. None of them wanted her.

Hawthorn handed Nory's duffel to Aunt Margo.

"What about a jacket?" Margo said. "Does she have a jacket?"

"Um," Hawthorn said.

"Get your jacket," Aunt Margo told Nory.

Nory did.

"Button it up."

Nory did.

"Say good-bye to Hawthorn and Dalia."

In a fog, Nory said good-bye.

"Hold on to my shoulders, now," Aunt Margo told Nory. "And whatever you do, don't let go."

The night air tingled on Nory's skin. The moon, just rising, glowed bright.

Down below, the towers of Sage Academy disappeared. Then the lights of Nory's hometown were gone, too.

Nory and Margo flew over black blobs that looked like forests, and black blobs that looked like buildings. The roads were lit up by streetlights and tiny cars.

At one point, a family of crows flew alongside them. Nory reached out to touch them but they swooped away.

Aunt Margo wasn't chatty. She was concentrating.

Eventually, they flew down to the lights of a small town built on a hillside. Little houses with porches were jammed up against one another, many of them brightly lit inside.

Aunt Margo landed in a yard full of flowers next to a very small, very old wooden house. A battered WELCOME! sign hung from the door.

"This is your new home," Aunt Margo said proudly. "Number 14 Clover Street in Dunwiddle." She pointed to the right. "Six blocks that way and four blocks over is Dunwiddle Magic School."

"What kind of school is it?" Nory said.

"It's a *school* school," said Aunt Margo. "A public school."

Nory's legs quivered.

"It's a nice place," Margo continued. "Not fancy

like Sage Academy, which I would argue is a good thing. Just a school where you'll learn lots and make friends and have fun."

"Oh," Nory said. "But will they know what to do with my—" She couldn't get the words out. *My messed-up magic?*

"Yes," Margo said. "They have a great new program geared toward students like you."

"Like me?"

"Well, not *exactly* like you, because there's only one Nory." Aunt Margo smiled at her, as if being the only Nory wasn't a bad thing. "But the school has just started a class for kids who struggle with magic. It's new this year! Isn't that exciting?"

Struggle with magic?

Oh, no.

Nory had heard rumors of programs like this. There were a few in New York City. One in Miami.

She was going to be in a particular class for the worst of the wonky.

"What's it called?" Nory asked. She had a bad feeling in her gut.

Aunt Margo walked up to the door of the house and unlocked it. "It's called Upside-Down Magic."

6

unt Margo had fixed up a tiny guest bed-
room for Nory. It had bright green walls and
an iron bed frame. There were no toys, no
art supplies, no family photographs. But there was a
stack of library books by the bed and a vase of late
summer roses on the desk.

In the morning, Aunt Margo showed Nory the rest
of the house. She explained how to work the remote
control for the television. She taped a chore schedule
on the fridge. Then they went to the grocery store,
where Aunt Margo asked Nory what her favorite

cereal was. Nory knew she should say Fiber Flakes, because that was Father's favorite. But Father wasn't here, was he? Father had sent Nory away, on purpose, so in a flash of recklessness she told her aunt the truth.

"Fruity Doodles."

Aunt Margo didn't blink. She bought two boxes of Fruity Doodles, as well as half a dozen apples and a pint of chocolate ice cream.

"I arranged for a neighbor boy to walk you to the first day of school tomorrow," Aunt Margo said over dinner. It was takeout pizza.

"Who is he?"

"His name's Elliott. I taxi his mom to work at the hospital a couple towns over," Aunt Margo said after swallowing a bite of pizza. "Her shift is early, so I'll be gone when you wake up. Can you fix yourself a bowl of Fruity Doodles?"

"Yes."

"And be sure to switch off the lights when you

leave. Oh, and Elliott's in the Upside-Down Magic class, too. That's pretty great, don't you think?"

No, Nory didn't think it was pretty great. There was nothing great about any part of the situation. But she knew Aunt Margo was being thoughtful. "What's Elliott's magic?"

"He's a Flare. And an unusual one, from what I've heard. I haven't seen him in action. He's—well, you'll see when you meet him. But he's a nice, nice boy. He'll swing by to get you at eight."

The next morning, Nory woke up to an empty house. It took her a moment to remember everything. When she did, her heart felt empty, too.

She looked on the bright side. Hawthorn wasn't there to make her wear a dress or braid her hair. That meant she could choose her own clothes.

Nory wiggled into her lucky purple pants, pulled on a hoodie, and left her hair big. She was dressed for school by seven thirty, which gave her plenty of time to eat breakfast, watch cartoons, and get really and totally terrified.

Would everyone else know one another from ordinary school?

What if no one spoke to her?

What if she didn't make any friends?

What if she *never* made any friends and she spent her lunches hiding in the girls' bathroom trying not to turn into a bitten?

The doorbell rang. Nory jumped, then answered the door. The boy on the steps was pale and tall, with nice straight teeth and long legs. He had big hair, too. Short loopy curls sprang over his head, defying gravity.

"Hi," said the boy. "I'm Elliott."

"Hi." Nory made herself smile.

"You've got a fake smile," Elliott observed. "But that's okay. So do I."

"What?"

"It's the first day of school. Der. *And* it's the first

day of Upside-Down Magic class. Everyone's going to be staring at us, and not in a good way."

Nory blinked.

"We are now officially wonkos," Elliott said. He shook his head. "I know some of the Upside-Down kids from before, and a few of them are scary. Others are just . . ."

Nory still couldn't find her words. Scary and wonky? Oh, why couldn't she just be at Sage Academy?

"Come on," Elliott said, jumping down Margo's front steps one at a time. "I've lived here all my life, so I know the quickest way to get there."

Is the quickest way really the best? Nory wanted to ask. But she didn't, so Elliott peppered her with questions instead. He was a talker.

"What's your favorite kind of ice cream?"

"Chocolate," Nory said. She and Dalia liked chocolate. Hawthorn liked peach. Father didn't eat sweets.

"What's your favorite animal?" Elliott asked.

"Dragon," Nory said. She had never seen one—although for a brief time she'd almost been one—but she was hoping to travel to Australia one day and see them in the wild.

"What's your favorite color?"

"Purple."

"I heard about your mixed-up animals from your aunt. Is it scary?"

Nory snapped to attention. He knew? Of course he knew. Father had told her aunt. Her aunt had told the school. That was how she'd gotten into the Upside-Down Magic class.

"Yeah, it's scary," she told Elliott.

"Can you do normal ones?"

"Sometimes."

"Why are you black when your aunt's white?"

"My dad's black. My mom was white."

"Do you want to tell me about your mom?"

"No, thanks," she said to Elliott. What could she tell him? What did she really know? She didn't remember much.

But he wouldn't stop. "Is she dead? I heard she was dead."

"Sounds like you already know."

"Want to tell me about your dad?"

"No."

"Want to tell me about *anything*?"

Sheesh. Nory was at a loss. She wasn't sure she wanted to open up yet. Or ever. But she didn't want to upset Elliott, either. He was the best chance she had of making a friend here.

"Knock, knock," she said.

He smiled. "Who's there?"

"Me."

"Me, who?"

"Knock, knock," she repeated.

"Who's there?"

"Me."

"Me, who?"

"Knock, knock."

"Who's there?"

"Meow."

"Meow, who?"

She grinned. "Just meow. I got bored waiting for you to answer the door so I turned into a cat."

Elliott paused. Thought.

And laughed.

He had a great laugh. Big and snorty.

They reached the top of the hill. There was a red brick building with kids milling around it. Elliott stopped and waved at it dramatically. "Here we are: Dunwiddle Magic School," he said. "And look, there's Andres. He'll be in our class *for sure.*"

Elliott tipped his big-hair head at a boy a few yards away, floating in the air. He was brown, probably Latino, Nory thought. He had shaggy hair and wore a stripy shirt. He was a Flyer, obviously, but he was much higher up than any beginner flyer Nory had seen. Every so often his body jerked forward. He flailed his arms. Around one ankle was a red rope. An older girl held the other end and chatted with her friends.

"Is he on a leash?" Nory whispered.

"That's his sister Carmen holding the other end," Elliott said. "Want to know what happened?"

Nory nodded.

"On the day before his tenth birthday, Andres flew up into the air during math. Just flew up. Not on purpose or anything. Our classroom had a ceiling fan. Andres went straight into it. His hair got caught. He spun around three times and then flew off into one corner. He hasn't been able to come down to the ground since. He has to sleep up on the ceiling, eat up there, everything. If he wasn't on the leash, he'd float away like a helium balloon."

This sounded awful. "Poor Andres."

"Yeah. No one hangs out with him anymore," said Elliott. "It's awkward."

"So, what's wrong with *you*?" Nory asked.

Elliott barked another laugh. "You mean, why am I in Upside-Down Magic?"

"Uh-huh."

"My problem is that I'm a Flare, only . . ." He broke off in the middle of his sentence and dragged

Nory behind a bush. "I don't like people to see," he whispered. "But you're gonna see it anyway in school. I might as well." Elliott picked up a twig and held it out at arm's length. A zap of light set the twig on fire.

Nory jumped back, not wanting to get burned. But there was no need. The twig flamed for only an instant. Then the light went out. The entire piece of wood crackled over with ice.

Ice!

"I flare but then it freezes," Elliott moaned. "Or else it doesn't flare at all."

Nory touched the ice twig and looked at Elliott in awe. She'd never known anyone who could freeze things before. She'd never even *heard* of people who could freeze things before.

"Come on, before the first bell rings," said Elliott, changing the subject. He dragged Nory out from behind the bush. "I hear the cafeteria food is gross. I hear the principal is invisible. I hear we get recess every day after lunch and you're not supposed to go in the wooded area. Still, everyone goes in there anyway. The lunch duty ladies don't pay good attention. Oh, and watch out for Pepper. Pepper will *definitely* be in our class, which is not good news."

"It's not?" Nory said. "Why?"

"Pepper's an Upside-Down Fuzzy—in other words, a Fierce. There have only been, like, two Fierces in all of history, I think. Extremely wonky. I know because I went to ordinary school with Pepper. On the day Pepper's powers came in . . . *pow!*"

Nory's heart thumped. "What happened?"

"Stampedes, howling, peeing on the carpet. Our neighbors have goats, and Pepper made them stampede through the fence. And I know these other people who used to have a pet dog. Pepper scared it so badly it hid for two weeks. Then when it finally came home, it was always trying to bite people. Pepper terrified that dog into permanent meanness. The people had to give the dog away."

"Wow." Nory shivered.

"I've heard other stories, too. Horses crying. Cats trying to hide in mouse holes."

"What do Fierces do to Fluxers?" she asked. "Like, if a Fluxer is in animal form and Pepper comes along?"

"Pepper terrifies them, just like any other animal."

"What if we're in our human form?"

"Dunno. It's probably still bad. I'm a human, and Pepper scares me," Elliott said.

Nory wasn't sure how she'd ever survive her class.

They were almost to the stairs leading to the school's front door when Elliott abruptly peeled off to the left. "Just saw my Flare friends from ordinary school," he said, talking over his shoulder. "I haven't seen them all summer, practically. They must miss me! You'll be okay, right? I'll see you in class."

Nory wasn't sure she'd be okay at all, but before she could even wave, Elliott had been swallowed by the crowd.

First day. So many students.

Just one Nory.

Okay. Deep breath. You can do this, Nory told herself. *It won't be that bad. Maybe it'll even be fun.*

She would look on the bright side.

Starting today, she was going to learn new things and make new friends.

I really, really will.

She held her head high and walked inside.

7

The hallways of Dunwiddle School were nothing like the friendly hallways of Nory's old ordinary school. And they were nothing like the elegant hallways of Sage Academy, either. The floors of Dunwiddle were linoleum. The walls were white and there were red fire extinguishers hanging every two yards. Large signs announced rules in big black letters:

NO FIRES EXCEPT IN THE FLARE LAB.

NO FLYING EXCEPT IN THE FLYERS' COURT

OR THE YARD.

VISIBLE HUMAN SHAPES TO BE USED IN THE

HALLWAYS AT ALL TIMES.

And: ANIMAL FRIENDS ARE NOT ALLOWED.

Not everyone was obeying these rules, however. Two big Fuzzy boys had mice peeking out of their jacket pockets. Several Flyers were hovering two feet off the floor, talking about their summer vacations. Nory turned a corner and nearly stumbled over three black kittens running away as if their lives depended on it.

They must have seen Pepper, she thought. *Poor little kittens.*

Ahead of her, she saw a water fountain. Then she didn't. It had disappeared. Then a girl walked by. A stream of water splurted from the invisible fountain and soaked the girl's shirt. She scowled and said to the air, "Jeremy Huang, I know that's you."

Nory couldn't see Jeremy Huang, but she could hear his laughter.

There didn't seem to be anybody around to stop him from playing the trick again.

Nory made a mental note to stay at least five feet away from every water fountain.

Dunwiddle felt like a maze. The deeper Nory went, the more lost she got. Where was she supposed to go? What was her classroom number again? Margo had told her before bed, but that seemed so long ago now. Nory couldn't remember.

A Flare girl with flaming candlesticks ran past, laughing deliriously. Nory jumped to the side. Then she turned a corner and had to duck fast as a bat nearly crashed into her head.

Ahhhh!

She hadn't been in school for more than ten minutes, and already she needed a break. She looked around and saw a door marked SUPPLY CLOSET.

Very cautiously, she opened the door and found . . . a nice, ordinary supply closet. *Phew.* She could rest there for a minute. Without anyone noticing, Nory slipped inside and let out a shaky sigh. It was dim, but not completely dark. There was a window at the top of the door. Nory saw brooms and mops and buckets in the back. Metal shelves lined the walls, stocked with cleaning products. There were about twenty fire extinguishers and way too many bags of cat litter.

Nory sank to the floor. She drew her legs to her chest and propped her arms on her knees.

Deep breath, she told herself again. *Look on the bright side. Remember?*

"Would you like a lemon drop?" a voice asked.

Nory's head snapped up. She peered into the shadows.

A girl stepped out from behind the mop. She was small and Asian-American with a sweet round face. She had thick black hair in two ponytails and wore a baggy denim dress. It looked like a hand-me-down.

The girl fished a lemon drop from a small yellow box and handed it to Nory. "Why are you hiding here?" she asked.

"It's my first day," Nory said lamely. She popped the lemon drop into her mouth. It was sour and good.

"Mine, too."

"And it isn't anything like my ordinary school," Nory explained. "It's so big. There are all these animals. And invisible water fountains. And a million fire extinguishers. A bat flew at my head. I got turned around and couldn't find my classroom."

The girl nodded. "I got locked in a locker," she said. "Three eighth-grade Flickers made me invisible. Then they tossed me in without anyone noticing. They just left me there."

"That's awful."

"Well, I'm very short," said the girl. "It's tempting, I suppose."

"How did you get out?"

The girl sighed. "Principal Gonzalez is a Flicker. He heard me banging on the locker. He opened it and made me visible again. Then he told me to go right to class, but I saw those same mean eighth graders coming down the hall, looking for more victims, so I ducked in here instead."

"I have to go to this class for wonky kids," Nory blurted, surprising herself. "Everyone else in the class is going to be wonky, too. Can you think of anything more terrible? The kids who are normal are going to make fun of us the whole year. I know it."

The girl nodded. "Upside-Down Magic. They put me in that class, too."

"They *did*? Why?"

The girl checked her watch. "Class starts in one minute," she said. She extended her hand and helped Nory up. "It'll be okay. Maybe. Come on."

They slipped out of the supply closet. Nory kept close to her new friend as they strode down the hall.

They stopped a few feet in front of a classroom. "Room 151," the girl said. "This is it. Ms. Starr's class."

Nory grabbed her arm. "Hey, watch out for a kid named Pepper," she whispered. "He's a Fierce, and there've only been two in the whole world. He's super dangerous, even to humans."

The girl looked shocked. "What?"

"We should sit together," said Nory. "Okay? We can protect each other. From Pepper."

The girl looked at her funny and opened the classroom door.

The room inside was bright and sunny, with eight desks on one side and a large carpeted area on the other. A stack of mats was rolled up in one corner, and a pile of yellow umbrellas leaned against the wall. A large cupboard with a glass door was filled with what looked like brightly colored sweaters. Another held art supplies. There was a bookshelf stuffed with paperbacks. A poster on the wall read: *Remember the kid who gave up? Neither does anyone else.*

There were still fire extinguishers all along the walls, but at least it was a cheerful room.

Ms. Starr walked toward them as they entered. She had perfect posture and bright lipstick. She had darker skin than Nory and wore her hair up in a bun. Her bright yellow cardigan matched a shirt with yellow polka dots. She ushered Nory and the girl with the lemon drops into the room.

"Our last two students!" she said. "Welcome, welcome. I am Ms. Starr."

Nory looked at her classmates. The eight desks were in two rows of four. Two girls and two boys sat in the front. Elliott was by himself in the back row. He gave Nory a quick wave. Nory smiled back. The three desks nearest to him were empty.

Andres floated on the ceiling with his red leash dangling down. One of the empty desks was probably his. That left two empty desks—one for Nory and one for the lemon drop girl. So everyone in the class was here. Eight desks, eight kids.

Nory studied the two boys in the front row, trying to figure out which one was Pepper. One was a large, freckled, blond boy with ruddy skin and thick eyebrows. Maybe even thuggish eyebrows. He wore a sports jersey. The other was a darker, wiry boy with short hair and a hole in his jeans. He slumped in his chair and spun a pencil in his fingers.

Nory guessed Pepper was the large, thuggish one. She was scared of him already.

Ms. Starr shook Nory's hand. "You're Elinor Horace, yes?"

"Yes. But I go by Nory."

"Class, say hello to Nory Horace."

"Hello, Nory Horace," they chorused.

Ms. Starr turned to the lemon drop girl. "And here you are, as well," she said. She smiled at the girl as if she already knew her and liked her. "Class, say hello to Pepper Phan."

"Hello, Pepper Phan."

Nory gulped.

Pepper?

Did Ms. Starr just say Pepper?

The thuggish boy wasn't Pepper the Fierce.

The girl with the lemon drops was Pepper the Fierce.

Nory's vision blurred and her heart sped up. Her body started to tingle.

Oh no, oh no, oh no.

Fur. Tail. Claws. Teeth.

There, in the first period of the first day of school, Elinor Boxwood Horace turned into a bitten.

8

Nory was a bitten for only a minute, but during that minute she got a lot done. She chewed up one of Ms. Starr's paperbacks and knocked over the sunflowers on her desk. She ran three times around the classroom and then decided to build another beaver lodge. It was only when Bitten-Nory tried to gnaw on Ms. Starr's chair leg that the metal taste snapped her back to her Nory self.

She was under her teacher's desk.

Please let this be a bad dream, she thought.

"What the zum-zum was *that*?" a voice asked.

swished through the air. "As for you guys, you're here because someone thinks you should be. Because someone called you wonky, or broken. Or worse."

"Nothing like a positive message to start the day," Elliott whispered to Nory.

"But guess what?" Ms. Starr's face broke into a grin. "I've been called wonky and different, too! And I speak from experience when I say: There are ways to make the most of your magic, whether it's typical or not. I am here to help you get in touch with your nature, to understand your emotions, and to develop skills. With these ideas in mind, I'd like to invite each of you to show us your magic."

Her manner was joyful, as if they were sharing a secret. A *good* secret.

She turned to the blond boy with the thuggish eyebrows, although perhaps his eyebrows weren't quite so thuggish after all. His eyes were round and earnest, and a tuft of hair stuck up from the top of his head. He actually looked nice, if nervous.

"Sebastian?" Ms. Starr said. "Would you like to go first? Say something about yourself and then share your magic."

Sebastian stood. His chair scraped the floor. "My name is Sebastian. I'm a kind of Flicker," he said. "Only I can't turn invisible. And I can't turn other things invisible, either."

"What do you do, then?"

"I see sound waves. They're invisible to most people."

"Are there sound waves coming from me?" Ms. Starr asked.

"If there weren't, you'd be dead." Sebastian looked startled when some of the kids laughed. "Why is that funny?" he asked. "Sound waves are *very important*. When you talk or breathe, or when your heart beats? Sound waves. They're zooming all over the room." He waved his hands wildly. "Zoom! They overlap a lot. It's pretty complex."

"What's the point?" asked the other boy in the

front row. Nory thought he sounded rude. Also, he wore a T-shirt with a skull and crossbones on it, and Nory imagined him picking out that shirt on purpose, so that people would know right away what kind of boy he was. The kind to wear a skull-and-crossbones T-shirt.

"Seeing sound waves," he went on. "What good does it do you?"

"They're all around us," said Sebastian.

"And?"

"I see other invisible things, too."

"Whatever," said the boy.

Nory felt depressed. First, Elliott had ditched her for his Flare friends.

Then the girl she liked turned out to be Pepper the Fierce.

Then she'd turned into a bitten in front of everyone.

The skull-and-crossbones boy was mean.

There wasn't much of a bright side to this day.

"Thank you, Sebastian," Ms. Starr said. "I know it's not easy to go first." She turned to the skull-and-crossbones boy. "Bax? Would you like to go next?"

"No."

Nory expected Ms. Starr to say that he had to, but instead she smiled sweetly. "No problem. I'll come back to you later. How about you, Elliott?"

Elliott stood. He shifted uneasily and patted down his big hair. "Flare," he said.

"Flare and . . . ?" Ms. Starr prompted.

"Flare and Freezer," said Elliott, his eyes down.

"Would you show us, please?" Ms. Starr looked genuinely excited. "Here. I have a glass of water. Would you like to freeze it?"

"I can do regular Flare stuff, too," said Elliott. "Some of it, anyway."

"You can do that later," said Ms. Starr. "Let's start with freezing the water."

Elliott waved a hand. The water iced over right away. Then the ice shot down Ms. Starr's hand and up her sweater.

"Elliott, stop!" she cried.

Elliott stopped before the ice reached her neck.

He covered his hands with his face. "It's really wonky! I'm sorry!"

"We don't say *wonky*," Ms. Starr corrected. "Remember? We say *different*. Boys and girls, Elliott is an Upside-Down Flare. Thinking about opposites is a great place to start understanding unusual magic."

She said all this while taking off her frozen yellow sweater and pulling a spare cardigan out of a cupboard. "I came prepared," she said cheerfully. "That's one of the things we learned in UDM teacher training."

She put on the new cardigan. It was bright orange. "Thank you for sharing that with us, Elliott. Now, Andres, are you ready?"

Everyone looked up.

"I think it's pretty obvious what my magic does," Andres said gloomily. With a grunt, he pushed off the ceiling. His body drifted a foot toward the floor, then flew back to the ceiling as if he were being jerked by a yo-yo string. He bounced a few times before coming to a stop.

The girl next to Nory raised her hand. She was light-skinned and wore her dark hair pulled back in a high ponytail. She was dressed in funky red-and-black-striped pants and big boots. In her ear, Nory spotted a hearing aid.

"What happens if you go outside?" the girl asked Andres.

"I'm on a leash. I'm sure you all saw my sister walking me to school."

"What would happen if she let go?" the girl persisted.

"I don't know, and I don't want to find out," Andres said.

What an awful magic to have, Nory thought. *At least when I turn into a bitten I can turn back.*

She had little time to feel sorry for him, though. Ms. Starr had moved on and Pepper was rising from her desk. She kept her eyes on the ground.

"It's fine, Pepper," Ms. Starr said. "Really."

Pepper hunched her shoulders. She said some-thing Nory couldn't make out.

"A demonstration would be best," Ms. Starr answered gently. "Do you need a volunteer? A Fluxer, perhaps, since your magic works on animals? I'll get some kids from the seventh-grade class."

She picked up the phone, and less than a minute later, two seventh graders came in the room. A boy and a girl.

Pepper sighed.

"We're all here for you, Pepper," Ms. Starr encour-aged. "Don't worry."

"All right. Do either of you do crocodile?" Pepper asked.

The seventh graders shook their heads. "That's really advanced," said the girl.

"How about a bear?"

"No large carnivores until the end of high school," said the boy.

"In fifth we mastered all different colors of kit-ten," the girl volunteered.

"I was hoping for something that wasn't little and cute," Pepper muttered. "The nicer the animal, the worse this makes me feel."

"Kittens are fine," Ms. Starr said. "Let's see."

As if she'd flipped a switch, both seventh graders transformed into teensy kittens: one orange and one calico.

They were really good kittens, Nory thought, feeling a little jealous. Perfect whiskers, perfect stripes and spots. Not a touch of dragon anywhere.

Moving slowly, Pepper knelt down to the kittens. She held out her hand the way a person does to cats when the person wants to say, *I'm safe. See? Come sniff me!*

The calico's tail stood straight up. Her legs went rigid. She yowled a horrible, high-pitched yowl, then fled the room in a blur.

The orange kitten cowered and hissed. He tried to escape by crawling up the wall, his tiny claws scrabbling at the white paint.

Pepper was clearly the scariest animal these kittens could imagine.

Ms. Starr cleared her throat. "All right. All right. Thank you for showing us your power, Pepper. Let them relax now."

"But I can't," said Pepper desperately. "I can't turn it on or off. They just hate me."

"Hmm," said Ms. Starr. "Pepper, would you mind going down the hall—way down the hall? Just until everyone calms down?"

Twin spots of color appeared on Pepper's cheeks as she slunk out of the room.

9

Things worth doing are usually hard," Ms. Starr
said. "But so what? We're not afraid of hard
work, are we?"

It had taken Ms. Starr and the seventh-grade
teacher ten minutes to coax the orange kitten down
from the top of the cupboard. The calico had fled
down the hall and out the door, but had luckily
been found underneath a radiator. Now things were
back to normal. Pepper had returned, and slumped
in her chair.

"I'm here to work with you. With *all* of you," Ms. Starr continued. She gave a short nod, as if that settled matters. "Marigold, you're next."

The girl with the hearing aid stood up. "I'm Marigold, and my parents live three hours away," she said. "I moved in with my grandparents so I could come to this program. My grandparents let me watch as much TV as I want, so that part's good. But I miss my family."

Me, too, Nory thought.

Marigold went on. "I'm not Upside-Down, exactly. I mean, not an opposite. I'm . . ."

Whatever Marigold was, she couldn't find the right words for it. Or else she didn't want to say them out loud.

"It's okay. Just show us your magic," Ms. Starr told her.

"If you say so." Marigold touched her chair. It began to shrink. Smaller and smaller until—oh! They couldn't see it anymore.

"I shrank my bed and now I have to sleep on an air mattress," Marigold said. "And I shrank my grandpa's car and now he has to use his bicycle. This year I hope I can learn how to make things big again. Or at least control the shrinkage."

"You're kidding," scoffed Bax, the rude boy who wouldn't show his magic. "You shrink things, which basically ruins them, and you don't know how to fix them?"

Ms. Starr clapped her hands. "She doesn't know how *yet*. That's something we can work on, Marigold."

Marigold bit her lip and nodded. Then, since her chair was too small to see, she sat down on the floor.

"Willa, you're next," said Ms. Starr.

The girl who rose from her desk was like a blond white elf, made of pointy elbows and knees. Her hair was a pale shiny curtain and her mouth was full of braces. "I make it rain," she said.

"Willa is another Upside-Down Flare," said Ms. Starr. "Elliott, isn't that interesting?"

"Can you light fires?" Elliott asked.

Willa shook her head. "No."

"Let's try to talk in positives," said Ms. Starr. "You do rain, at present, and I'm sure you'll do more as you develop. Do we need umbrellas?"

Willa nodded.

"Again, I am prepared!" Ms. Starr proclaimed. She strode to the group of yellow umbrellas leaning in the corner. Then she handed one to each student.

"We're ready, Willa!" she called out.

Nory felt her depression lift a little. If Willa could make rain, that was important. She could help crops grow, bring plants to barren deserts. Help animals. A rain talent could be really *useful*. It might be very unusual, but no one could fairly call it wonky.

She got her umbrella open just in time. Rain poured from the ceiling, drenching the room and running in small rivers from everyone's umbrellas.

"The floor's wet," said Elliott.

"And the carpet," said Marigold.

"And all our papers," said Bax. "And the books."

"It's kind of awesome, though," Nory murmured, admiring a raindrop on the toe of her sneaker.

"Is it?" said Andres. "Really?" His umbrella was inverted and filled with rain. It had become heavy and was pulling his upper body down while his feet stayed on the ceiling. He was soaked.

Willa turned the rain off. "Sorry," she said. "It never ends well. I can only do it indoors, so it's kinda worthless."

"Positives, remember?" said Ms. Starr. "Every day is an adventure, and Willa has a remarkable and unusual talent. We'll get the janitor in here, and Andres, I'll see if I can get you dry clothes."

She picked up the classroom phone and made a call. After she hung up, she said, "Problem solved. But let's all bring in spare things to keep in our lockers, okay? The days will go smoother that way, with Willa and Marigold and Elliott among us. The Flare classrooms all have to do the same, you know—and they need burn ointment! So we should count ourselves lucky."

"I can totally light fires," said Elliott. "You just didn't give me a chance to show it."

Everyone closed their umbrellas and stood awkwardly around the wet desks.

"It's down to you, Bax," said Ms. Starr, smiling at the one student who hadn't yet shown his magic. "Are you ready to share?"

"No," Bax said.

"Come on, Bax," Ms. Starr said. She was firm but friendly. "We will all support you, and we will help you become your best self. The spirit of the UDM classroom is trust."

"I don't think I should," Bax insisted.

"I disagree. We can start by talking. I know from your papers that you're an unusual Fluxer, like Nory. Right?"

"Um."

"Nory showed us a very interesting"—Ms. Starr gave Nory a smile—"what was it?"

"A bitten," said Nory. "A beaver-kitten."

"A *lovely* bitten," said Ms. Starr. "And after that, I think we're prepared to handle anything. So? Bax?"

Bax cradled his head in his hands.

"Whenever you're ready," Ms. Starr said.

"Fine," he mumbled.

Nory heard a *whoosh* as Bax turned into a tremendous chunk of rock. The floor shook as he crashed off his chair and onto the floor.

"Whoa," Willa said.

"That was a great sound wave," Sebastian added.

"He's a *rock*," Nory said, astonished. She had never known a Fluxer to become a rock, a plant, or anything that wasn't an animal. She couldn't quite believe it.

"He's really something!" said Ms. Starr. She hopped off her desk and walked around Bax, admiring the thoroughness of his transformation. "Very good, Bax. All rock, no boy. How do you feel?"

Bax just sat there.

Ms. Starr laughed. "Okay, you've proved your point. Change back, please."

Bax just sat there.

"Bax?" Ms. Starr shook him. "Fiddlesticks, I think he's stuck."

It took four people to roll him down the hallway to the medical office. Nurse Riley was a pudgy gentleman who wore scrubs decorated with unicorns. He seemed surprised to see Bax, but confident. He promised to have him fixed up before lunch was over.

Nory followed the rest of her classmates on the way to the cafeteria. *This is Upside-Down Magic class,* she thought. *A Freezer, a Fierce, a girl who shrinks things, a girl who wets things, a boy who sees sound waves, two wonky Fluxers, and a Flyer who can't come down from the ceiling.*

Nory took her hundredth deep breath of the day.

She wanted to look on the bright side . . . but from where she was standing, she didn't see much of one, at all.

In the cafeteria, Nory and Elliott both got plates of mac and cheese. At the salad bar, Elliott got only cucumbers. Nory got only cherry tomatoes. He was a single-veggie guy and she was a single-veggie girl. Well, tomatoes were not *really* veggies—as Father liked to point out—but close enough. Plus they both had big hair. Nory smiled at that thought. Single veggies and big hair: two things, at least, that they had in common besides Upside-Down Magic.

"Come sit with my Flare friends from ordinary school," Elliott offered. Nory nodded and followed him to a table where two girls and a boy sat, already eating. The two girls had carrots *and* celery *and* broccoli next to their mac and cheese. The boy had a huge serving of mac and cheese and zero vegetables.

"Hi, guys," Elliott said, setting down his tray. "This is Nory. She just moved to town." He gestured at the others. "Nory, this is Lacey, Zinnia, and Rune. We call ourselves the Sparkies."

The girl named Lacey looked familiar. Nory drew her eyebrows together and said, "This is going to sound weird, but do I know you?"

"No, you don't *know* me," Lacey replied coolly. "But you've *bothered* me."

Zinnia tried to smother a giggle. She didn't try very hard.

Nory took a spot at the table. She studied Lacey more closely.

Sharp, short haircut.

Tiny feet and hands.

Enormous black glasses with lenses the size of large cookies.

"Oh!" Nory exclaimed. "We were in line together at the Sage Academy test! You didn't get in either!"

Lacey made a scornful sound, stabbed a piece of broccoli, and said, "Please. Of course I got in."

"But . . ."

"I decided not to go," Lacey said. "I wanted to stay in Dunwiddle and do Flare stuff with my besties."

Nory opened her mouth to reply, then thought better of it. She remembered Lacey's father coaching her on roasting marshmallows. She remembered Lacey's panic when her name was called, and her sobs as she fled the hall.

Lacey chewed the piece of broccoli. She chewed it so aggressively that it seemed a small act of war. Then she swallowed and said, "I heard about *you*, though. The headmaster's daughter, too wonky to get into her own father's school."

Nory felt punched in the gut. She said, "We don't say *wonky*. It's unkind. We say *upside down*."

"Ha," Zinnia said.

"Love it," Rune said. "Adorable."

Elliott turned red and looked down at his plate. "Hey! Guys! Remember that food fight in fourth grade? With the hamburgers?"

"Epic," said Rune.

"Well, for fourth graders," Zinnia corrected.

"Things are different now," said Lacey. "We're the Sparkies."

"I know," Elliott said. "I came up with that name. Duh."

"And it's the perfect name—for *us*," Lacey said. She pointed to Rune, Zinnia, and herself. "*We* are the Sparkies. You turned out to be . . . an icy?" She laughed, and her friends laughed with her.

Elliott's smile dimmed.

"You need to go now," Lacey said. She took a bite of a baby carrot. "You're embarrassing yourself and you don't even know it."

"And when you embarrass yourself, you embarrass us," Zinnia said pleasantly.

Elliott turned to Rune, looking for some support.

"Well . . ." Rune mumbled.

"Rune," Lacey said.

Rune rubbed the back of his neck. "We've been trying to ditch you all summer. Sorry, dude."

"We tried to tell you nicely, but you wouldn't listen," Zinnia said.

Lacey took a dainty sip of milk. "That's why we had to melt your bike tires."

Rune chuckled. "Epic."

Elliott's head snapped back. "That was you?" he asked. "Wow. Yeah. Epic is right." He tried to force a smile. "That bike thing, I never would have guessed."

"So leave us alone already," said Lacey. "Honestly, Elliott, you can be so dense. No wonder you got put in UDM."

A familiar tingle shivered up Nory's spine. Her vision blurred.

No, no, no! Stay human. Do not flux in the lunchroom.

But it was too late. Nory was out of her chair and on the floor. Her hands weren't hands anymore. They were covered in thick black fur, with sharp claws.

Oh, drat.

She knew this animal. She had done it before.

She was a skunk.

Step away. Just leave them alone, thought Girl-Nory.

But Skunk-Nory didn't step away. She was too angry at the Sparkies. How dare they be so mean to Elliott?

They were enemies. Hairless enemies. And she was a skunk! She could do stuff to enemies.

Bad stuff. Smelly stuff.

No, no! Girl-Nory thought, but it was no use.

Skunk-Nory began to swell. She grew big to match the size of her hairless enemies. Then she grew bigger and bigger, until—

A trunk popped out of her face. An elephant trunk.

Nory waved it menacingly in the air. She was Skunkephant-Nory! Body of a skunk, nose and size of an elephant!

And she was mad. So mad. She lifted her giant skunk tail.

"Nory! Stop!" Elliott shouted.

Skunkephant-Nory turned her haunches toward the hairless enemies.

"No! Don't!" Elliott cried.

She aimed her Skunkephant-Nory bottom.

"NORY! DO NOT SPRAY THE SPARKIES!"

Now one of the hairless things was tugging on her trunk. Skunkephant-Nory shook it off. It danced back in front of her and said, "Nory! It's me, Elliott. Don't do this!"

Elliott. She remembered Elliott. He was nice. He had walked her to school. He was a single-veggie guy.

"You can turn back," Elliott said. "I know you can, before anything too disgusting happens."

Okay, good idea, Girl-Nory thought. *I can do this. I will just change back. I will not spray anybody.*

But then, *WHAT WAS THAT?* Right in front of her was a tiny hairless thing in a baggy denim dress and two ponytails. It was the most terrifying thing she'd ever seen!

Ahhhhh! It was coming her way!

"Pepper, get out of here!" Elliott shouted. "You're *Fiercing!*"

DANGER! DANGER! HERE LIES DANGER!

Skunkephant-Nory reeled. Terror took over.

Elliott tried one more time. "Get away, Pepper! Stop, Nory!"

But it was too late. Skunkephant-Nory lifted her giant bushy tail and sprayed.

11

The cafeteria was closed until further notice.

The Sparkies were sent to the medical office. They had been sprayed so thoroughly that an actual fog surrounded them.

Rumor had it Nurse Riley fainted from the smell.

Thanks to Elliott, Pepper had jumped for cover just in time.

Nory had turned human again in the middle of the chaos, and before anyone could find her, or yell at her, or take her to the nurse, she ran down the hall to the supply closet and hid.

She was so mad at the Sparkies.

And very, very embarassed.

And sorry.

But she couldn't hide forever. After waiting a few minutes to calm down, she took a deep breath and walked out to recess alone. She would have to face everybody eventually, and it might as well be now.

In the yard stood a swing set and a big climbing structure. On the blacktop was a basketball court, where ten or so Flyers played fly-ball, hovering two feet up in the air. In a grassy area nearby, Fluxers turned into kittens and chased one another around. Some kids were doing ordinary stuff like jumping rope and playing tag.

"There's no fire and no flickering in the yard!" said one of the lunch ladies as Nory walked outside. "And only nonthreatening transformations! Understood?"

The UDM kids were standing around the swing set, with Sebastian holding on to Andres's leash. A larger group of ordinary kids were staring and pointing at them.

"Bunch of wonkos."

"They could have hurt someone!"

"That was really gross."

"Why do they have to be in our school?"

"Is it even safe?"

The UDM kids did their best to ignore the comments. Willa and Pepper were on the swings. Marigold pushed them alternately. Elliott and Bax bounced a basketball back and forth. When Nory walked over to them, the swings slowed to a halt. Everyone glared at her.

"I can't believe you did that to us," Elliott hissed. "You made us look like wonkos—"

"Dangerous wonkos!" Willa added.

"—in front of the entire school."

"I'm sorry," Nory said. "I didn't mean to!"

Willa and Pepper got off their swings, and they all turned their backs on her. Even Sebastian and floating Andres.

Tears pricked Nory's eyes. "You guys! Please!"

Not one of them talked to her. Not one of them looked at her. For the whole rest of the day, they pretended she didn't exist.

Ms. Starr lectured everyone about tolerance and forgiveness. She reminded them that they all had magical powers that sometimes got out of hand. "That's why we're here," she said. "If we can't count on one another, who can we count on?"

No one listened.

Nory called home when she got to Aunt Margo's. But no one answered.

"Please call me back," she said to the voice mail. "I can't stay here. I really can't."

She watched the phone. It didn't ring.

Aunt Margo got home from work just before dinnertime. "Let's call for pizza," she said to Nory. "Should we get olives on it? Or pepperoni?"

Nory was surprised. Hawthorn cooked something nutritious involving vegetables every night, and they all ate it in the dining room with cloth napkins. Then Nory and Dalia did the dishes before anyone was allowed dessert. "Pizza again?" she said.

"Do you eat meat?" asked Margo, looking at a takeout menu. "I realize I don't even know if you eat meat." She opened the fridge. It had some fruit and milk in it, but nothing that could be made into dinner. "Yes, pizza again. Definitely. The only other place that delivers is the fancy Japanese place and it's—well, it's not in the budget."

"Do you eat pizza every night?" asked Nory.

Aunt Margo flushed suddenly. "Don't you like pizza? I thought all kids wanted to eat pizza for every meal."

"I like pizza," said Nory. "It's fine."

Margo looked relieved. "We could each eat an apple before it gets here," she said. "So we get some vitamins. Sound okay?"

"Sure," said Nory.

"What about the meat?" said Margo, picking up her phone.

"Meat is good. You can go to town on the meat."

Margo ordered a small pizza with double pepperoni and they sat on the couch and ate their apples in silence while waiting for the delivery. Nory did her math and English homework. Margo looked over her taxi schedule for the next week on the computer.

Nory wanted to talk to someone about Pepper and the bitten and the skunkephant and the Sparkies and how everyone in Upside-Down Magic hated her guts now, but she had long ago learned not to talk about her wonky magic at home. Anyhow, she didn't know Aunt Margo well, and Margo seemed absorbed in the taxi schedule, so Nory stayed quiet.

There was just a living room and an eat-in kitchen. Nothing was very neat and nothing very messy. Margo didn't have much stuff, and she clearly wasn't interested in decorating. The living room had some grown-up books, a desk area with all her taxi papers piled around it, some cozy chairs, and a couch—but there were no board games, no pets, no art supplies or family photos. None of the jolly clutter that

Hawthorn and Dalia created in the back rooms of Father's house. None of the matching, careful quality of the formal front rooms.

Aunt Margo lived alone till I got here, Nory realized. She knew that already, of course, but suddenly she *felt* it.

There was a knock on the door and Margo got up to pay for the pizza. When she came back with the box, she flipped on the television.

They ate without plates, just a roll of paper towels, and watched the news. It was extremely boring. Aunt Margo didn't seem to realize it was boring, though. She leaned forward and shoved pizza in her mouth almost without stopping. "Flying with passengers is very physical," she said during a commercial. "I need a lot of food at the end of the day."

"Oh."

They watched another news segment and finished their pizza. Then Margo looked at Nory's face, really looked at her for the first time since she'd gotten home. She switched off the TV. "You had a bad first day, didn't you?"

Nory's throat closed up suddenly. She nodded.

"Super rotten bad, or just ordinary new-kid bad?"

Nory wasn't going to cry. She couldn't cry in front of this near-stranger aunt, the aunt who didn't even know how bad of a wonko Nory was yet, who had been so nice to take Nory in when her own father didn't want her. She just pressed her lips together to keep the crying in.

"Are you going to yak?" shouted Margo suddenly. "Oh, dear, don't yak on the carpet. Let's just walk you over here to the floor." She pulled Nory gently by the elbow until they were standing on a patch of bare floor. "Okay, yak here. Go right ahead, this is good yak territory. Watch out for your shoes."

Nory burst out laughing. "I'm not going to yak," she said.

"You're not?"

"No."

"Really?"

"Really."

Margo smiled. "Oh, phew, I thought that was your about-to-yak face."

"No."

"I thought the double pepperoni was a bad idea, maybe."

"No, no, it was good pepperoni."

"You made me a little nervous there," said Margo. "That face."

"No, no. It was—that was my super-rotten-bad-day face," Nory admitted.

"Oh." Margo looked at her expectantly.

There was a silence, and then Nory blurted, "I hurt a girl's feelings but not on purpose and I didn't know how to say sorry and then I turned into a bitten and ate some books and people thought that was weird but then at lunch I turned into a skunkephant and they had to close the cafeteria and it was really badly smelly like no smell you ever sniffed and I couldn't help it and Elliott's mad at me and the Sparkies are mad at me and the whole Upside-Down class is mad at me and they think I'm the wonkiest kid in the whole wonky classroom."

Aunt Margo sat down on the edge of the sofa. "Zamboozle," she said, finally. "That is a super rotten day to end all super rotten days, I think."

"Yeah."

"Okay. How can I help?"

Father always told his children they had to help themselves. He couldn't do things for them or make things easier. Helping themselves was the way they would learn. Nory kind of thought he was right about that—but it was nice to hear these words from Margo now.

"I don't know," Nory squeaked in reply.

"Then let's go for a fly," said Margo, pulling her coat from the closet. "Come on. Bundle up."

"Aren't you tired?"

"Not anymore. I got rest. I ate pizza. Here, wear some gloves."

They bundled up and went outside into Margo's backyard. Then they levitated straight up in the air together, not too high, and from there floated gently over the town of Dunwiddle. Margo pointed out the pharmacy, a street full of restaurants and shops, and the park with its pond full of ducks. A few other Flyers passed by, enjoying the evening light. One of them had a canary on a long leash, taking her for an outing. The others were alone, since most Flyers couldn't take passengers. Margo waved at them and called out, "It's my niece, Nory! The one I told you about!" Nory waved, too, and the Flyers waved back. Margo seemed proud of her. Or at least glad to have her.

They flew along a creek that meandered through town. They flew out over the town swimming pool, which was empty, and the fly-ball court at the high school.

After a while, they came back to Margo's house. They took hot showers and put on pajamas and then

Nory went to sleep in her little iron bed in the room with the bright green walls.

Much to her own surprise, she felt okay.

But the next morning at school was just as bad as the first day. "Today we're going to do math and geography and vocabulary just like any other class," Ms. Starr said. "But I like to get creative with literature." She smiled. "You're not just going to read poems and write essays. You're going to read poems and do interpretive dance."

"Huh?" said Elliott.

"Part of developing your Upside-Down Magic is getting in touch with your emotions. You want to understand your feelings so you don't—well, you know, turn into a bitten. Or a rock. Or cause a rainstorm when you don't want one. Or shrink someone's car. UDM is not about controlling your feelings, it's about understanding them!"

"Whatever," grumbled Bax. "I don't have feelings."

Then he turned into a rock and had to be taken to Nurse Riley. Marigold took him in a wheelbarrow Ms. Starr had brought to class that morning for this very purpose.

The rest of the students read a poem called "The Lost Mermaid." Then Ms. Starr played ocean music through the speakers and called them to the carpeted area of the classroom. "She can't find her parents! Feel her sadness!" cried Ms. Starr. She dropped to her knees and made swimming motions with her arms. "Feel her panic! Feel her terror! Feel whatever it is the poem made you feel! Get in touch with it!"

"I didn't sign up for a dance class," whined Andres from the ceiling.

"Give it a chance," said Ms. Starr. "You can be a hungry shark if you want to! Or an angry shrimp! Or a stoic rock. On second thought, don't be a rock. We never want to make fun of Bax."

"There are no such things as mermaids," Willa grumbled.

"Not true," Ms. Starr said. "No one has seen one for over a hundred years, but they did exist."

Sebastian rolled around on the carpet, apparently feeling feelings.

Pepper scrunched into a ball with her head between her knees.

Nory pretended to be a sad seaweed. She swayed over to Elliott, waving her hands swishily above her head.

"I'm really, really sorry," she said to him. "About the skunkephant. And your Sparkie friends."

"Go away," Elliott said. "I'm very busy being a blobfish."

"A blobfish?" Nory studied Elliott. He was leaning against the wall, not doing a thing.

Elliott became even more blob-like. "Yes, and I am feeling annoyed. I wonder if you can guess why."

"Because blobfish look like they're made out of dough?" Nory asked hopefully.

"Nope. That's not why." He scowled. "You're not

going to turn into a blob-kitten now, are you? A blitten?"

Nory shivered. Gross. "I can't make any promises," she said. "But I'll try not to."

Just then, the ceiling opened and rain poured down on all of them.

A lot of rain.

"Sorry!" yelled Willa.

"No need to apologize," cried Ms. Starr, running to grab the umbrellas. "This is a teachable moment! Let's talk about *why* that rain just happened. Let's understand the connection between your feelings and your magic."

The rain stopped.

Everyone got their spare clothes from their cubbies, and the janitor was called in again. But even though it was Willa who had caused the problem, it was still Nory that no one wanted to talk to.

The days passed, and nothing got better. When it came time for the class to study magic, Ms. Starr told her students to do headstands. They all had to come to the rug, where Ms. Starr urged them to flip their worlds upside down. She had Andres stand on his feet, like a bat, with his head downward. She gave him a closed umbrella as a prop.

No one except Willa was very good at it. Most of the students had to lean against the wall.

Bax turned into a rock every time he went upside down.

Every single time. Then he was taken off to Nurse Riley in the wheelbarrow. After about an hour, he'd return to class in his human form, usually with a green medicine mustache.

It seemed like a hopeless cause, but Ms. Starr made all of them keep practicing.

"Headstands calm our brains and relieve stress," she insisted. "More importantly, they let you see things upside down. They give you another way of thinking about the world. It really helps those of us with upside-down magic, I promise!"

Nory wasn't sure the teacher knew what she was

talking about. "Ms. Starr?" she asked one day when they were all upside down (except Bax, who was a rock, and Sebastian, who was on wheelbarrow duty). "Did headstands help you with your magic?"

Ms. Starr was in the center of the carpet, doing a perfect headstand. "It helped me tremendously," she said.

"Because your magic is Upside-Down, too," said Marigold.

"Absolutely. That's why I wanted to become a teacher."

"Just tell us what it is," begged Willa. "Please? We know it's different. But different *how*?"

"It's a magic that—well, it might disrupt the classroom, when I bring it in," said Ms. Starr, mysteriously. "I want us all to get settled before I share it with you."

"I bet you're a special kind of Flicker," guessed Elliott.

"No, some kind of Fluxer," guessed Andres.

"No, a Fuzzy," guessed Pepper.

"I'll tell you when it's time," said their teacher. "Now I want all of you to come down to the floor. Andres, I'll get that bag of bricks for you to hold. We're going to do a group trust exercise."

Everyone groaned.

Every day, as soon as school let out, Nory raced to Aunt Margo's and called home.

Every day she reached the voice mail.

"Please call me back, Father," she said.

"It's awful here, Hawthorn," she said. "And I miss your cooking."

"The other kids talk about me when they think I can't hear, Dalia," she said. "They're all really messed up. I just want to come home. Please?"

No one called back.

Two weeks after Nory arrived, on a Saturday morning, Aunt Margo made a call of her own.

"Stone," she said sharply, "I know you're there. I know you're letting our calls go to voice mail. I'm sure you've told Hawthorn and Dalia not to pick up. This is unacceptable. Nory is your daughter. You need to stop acting like a dimwit. I know you have my number, so call us back."

But Father didn't.

After two hours of waiting, Aunt Margo punched in a different number. "It's time for you to meet Nory," Aunt Margo said to the person on the phone. "Can you come get us?" She paused, then said, "Yes. Perfect. Give us five minutes. Six if you want me to brush my hair." She laughed, said, "Love you, too," and hung up.

"We're going out for lunch," she told Nory. "Figs is coming for us in his car."

"Who's Figs?" Nory asked. She was crumpled on the couch feeling sorry for herself.

"He's my boyfriend. You'll adore him. He's taking us to this new bakeshop that two of our Flare friends just opened. The cinnamon rolls are supposed to be wonderful. You can handle a cinnamon roll for lunch, right?"

"Maybe." Nory smiled for the first time that day. Father always insisted on vegetables and protein for lunch, so no one got weighed down with too much sugar and starch. "But what if Father calls back? Or Hawthorn, and we aren't here to pick up?"

"Piffle," said Margo. "I'll take my cell. Figs is already on the way. Oh, there he is!"

A large brown-and-white dog jumped through an open window in the living room, barking and wagging his tail.

"Figs!" Aunt Margo scolded. "Stop showing off, you big hairball." She turned to Nory. "Figs has been wanting to show you his Saint Bernard since the first day you got here. He just got it licensed. But I told him to wait. I wanted you to have a chance to get settled."

Figs bounded over to Nory and grinned a doggy grin. Then he backed up and shook his body so that his fur stood out all over. A moment later he changed into a broad-shouldered, olive-skinned man. He wore jeans and a black T-shirt, and had a big smile. "Hello, Nory," he said, reaching out his hand. "I'm Figaro Russo. I run the pharmacy in town. We've got aspirin, wart medicine, burn ointment, catnip, you name it. We sell candy, too. You should come by and spend your allowance. You're giving her an allowance, right, Margo? She needs one."

"Fine," said Margo. "I'll give her an allowance. Now can we go? I'm starving."

"Let's do it," Figs said, clapping his hands. "Cinnamon rolls, here we come!"

They had a wonderful lunch of starch, grease, and sugar. Figs talked about fluxing a lot. He was licensed for four different dog shapes.

"Never could get my kitten right, though," he said, encouragingly. "I must be the only Fluxer in North America without a cat license. And I haven't got any large carnivores, either. But oh, well. What would I do with them, anyway? Dogs just come more naturally to me. I'm working on chihuahua. I think it might be useful to do a really little dog. But so far, no luck."

On the way home in Figs's van, Aunt Margo's cell rang. She looked at it, raised her eyebrows, and handed it to Nory.

Nory's heart jumped. She put the phone to her ear. "Hello?"

"Nory! We're on speakerphone!" Dalia said.

"Who's on speakerphone?" Nory asked.

"Me and Hawthorn."

"What about Father?"

"At a meeting," Dalia said. "You know Father. Always working, even on the weekends."

"Hi, Nory," Hawthorn said. "Sorry it's taken us this long to call you back. Father wanted us to let you get settled first. But after Aunt Margo's message, we decided we should sneak a call."

Well, it's about time, Nory almost said. But she didn't. What if they hung up?

She would make the best of things. She would.

"Aunt Margo just took me to a really nice lunch," she said. "It had no vegetables at all."

"Lucky," said Dalia.

"How's the house?" Hawthorn asked. "Is your room very small?"

"How's your new school?" asked Dalia. "Is it depressing?"

"We want you back," Hawthorn swore. "It's just hard to convince Father."

"But we have an idea!" Dalia added. "We thought if you could get control of the animal bodies, you know, so you don't chew things and set things on fire—"

"And if you can get yourself doing a really good kitten without any weird things popping out—"

"Father said your kitten was really *good* until it went wonky."

"—then you could get yourself tested out of that Upside-Down Magic class. You could go to a class for normal kids!" said Hawthorn. "Then you could work on being *more* normal, and reapply to Sage Academy."

"Reapply?" said Nory. On the other end of the line, she heard the faint sound of a door being opened. "Is that Father?"

"Oh, no," Dalia said, her voice going up in pitch. "We have to go."

"Get out of that special class," Hawthorn said. "Just stop being wonky, and come home. We miss you."

"Hawthorn? Dalia?" Nory heard her father say. "Who is that on the phone?"

There was a click, and then nothing.

Nory squeezed her eyes shut in the back of the van. Figs and Aunt Margo were talking about whether they could make cinnamon rolls at home. Aunt Margo was saying the recipe sounded too hard and they should just make cinnamon toast like everyone else did. Figs was saying you shouldn't avoid trying something just because it was hard.

Nory only half listened.

She was thinking about Hawthorn and Dalia's plan.

First she had to learn to be normal. Yes. Then she'd get out of Upside-Down Magic and be put into regular Fluxer class. She'd learn to be even more normal in Fluxer class and then she'd reapply to Sage Academy. She could even do fifth grade over again. She wouldn't mind.

If Nory could do all that—if Nory could be *normal*—surely Father would let her come home.

12

On Monday, Bax turned into a rock at the beginning of headstand practice. As usual.

It was Nory's turn to take him to Nurse Riley, and as she pushed the wheelbarrow down the hall, she peered into the other classrooms. It was the hour for magic study, and the fifth-grade Flares were roasting marshmallows in their hands.

Their classroom smelled delicious.

The Fuzzy class stood in a circle around a large silver unicorn. They were grooming it and feeding it carrots.

The fifth-grade Flyers were levitating two feet above the floor, slowly going round in a circle. Every now and then, one of them drooped lower or tipped backward, and the teacher would blow a whistle. Young Flyers were called earlybirds. Most of them wouldn't be able to go higher than five feet until high school.

Andres was an exception, obviously. Andres could probably soar all the way to the moon if he wanted, but then what? He wouldn't be able to get back down.

Nory walked on. She reached the medical office and said, "We're here," to Bax, even though she wasn't sure he could hear her.

"Ah," Nurse Riley said. "Headstand practice again?"

Nory passed over the handles of the wheelbarrow. "Can I watch? Please?"

"Believe me, doll, this is something you don't want to see," Nurse Riley said. He shut the door.

Nory took a different route back to Ms. Starr's room. The Flicker classroom had a room full of kids staring at toads that hopped about on their desks.

"Begin!" cried the teacher. Half the toads went invisible. The other half looked like they were missing various toad body parts. No feet, no face, no middle. It was actually kind of cool, Nory thought.

The fifth-grade Fluxers were working on kittens. It wasn't a big class, since Fluxers were rare. There were only ten students. Nory could see they were trying to add colors to their kitten transformations. Four were still just black, but five had white spots, and one was successfully calico. "Luciana, stop looking out the window," the teacher chided. "The squirrels aren't your concern. And Alastair, don't scratch the furniture. All of you, remember to keep control of the animal mind!"

Nory wanted more than anything to join them.

When she got back to the classroom, everyone was still doing headstand practice. Soothing music played. Ms. Starr stood upright in the center of the carpet.

Nory chose a spot beside Elliott. "Elliott," she whispered. "Hey! Elliott!"

He pretended not to hear her.

"Boys and girls, think about this," Ms. Starr said. "When you are upside down, the ceiling becomes the floor and the floor becomes the ceiling. Am I right?"

"Bor-ring," Marigold said under her breath.

"Fine," Ms. Starr said, piercing Marigold with her gaze. "But if you want to be the best you can be, this is how."

She walked over and devoted herself to coaxing Andres into his proper bat position.

"I have a plan for us," Nory whispered to Elliott. "And I know you can hear me, so stop pretending."

"You're annoying me again," said Elliott.

"It's a good plan," said Nory. "A plan to get us out of Upside-Down Magic."

Elliott pressed his lips together.

"You and I are different than the others in our class," Nory whispered. "We could do magic like normal people if we just got enough practice."

Elliott didn't stop her, so Nory went on.

"If you can stop freezing things and I can stick to just regular animals, then we can transfer out of UDM. We can go to the normal classes."

"You skunk-sprayed the Sparkies," said Elliott.

"I'm *sorry*."

"They were my best friends until that happened."

Were they? Nory wondered. But she didn't want to say that to Elliott. Instead, she said, "You can practice your flare talent, and I'll practice my fluxing. We can help each other."

"If I were a regular Flare," mused Elliott, "maybe they'd like me again."

"We'll work on it!" Nory whispered. "You and me, after school."

Elliott rolled out of his wobbly headstand and patted down his curls. "Will Ms. Starr let us leave this class? Will Principal Gonzalez?"

This was something Nory hadn't considered. "Of course they will," she said. "They have to."

"Do they?"

"We can at least ask, can't we?" Nory argued.

They waited until the end of the school day. As soon as the other UDM kids left, they approached Ms. Starr's desk.

"Yes?" Ms. Starr said, looking confused about why they were still there. She also looked tired, and Nory realized she was wearing her fourth change of clothes that day.

"We just wanted to say that you're a really good teacher," said Nory. "And Andres and Willa and everyone, they're all nice. Right, Elliott?"

Elliott blinked.

"But Elliott and I, we're not the same as the others in this class," Nory went on. "We can do normal magic, if we practice. They can't."

"Is that so?" Ms. Starr said.

"Yes, it is. But we need your help. So will you?"

"Will I what?"

Nory stood up straighter. "We want to be tested. Please. To see if we can place into the regular fifth grade."

Ms. Starr's face fell. "Why?"

Nory felt a pang. She hadn't meant to hurt Ms. Starr's feelings.

"Because we don't want to be wonkos," Elliott blurted.

"I hope no one is using that word here at Dunwiddle," Ms. Starr said, frowning.

If Elliott heard the tremble in Ms. Starr's voice, he didn't let on. "We just want a chance to be normal," he said.

"Helping you be normal isn't my job," Ms. Starr said. Her expression was earnest. "My job is to help you understand what you have and accept it. I am teaching you how to make the most of your talents. This class is where you belong, because you have something unusual to offer."

"Please," begged Nory.

"Did you know that in the olden days, unusual powers were prized?" Ms. Starr continued. "Powers like making rainstorms, creating ice, or seeing what no one else could see. Turning into combination animals was considered beautiful."

"They used to think Upside-Down Magic was better than regular magic?" Elliott asked.

"Some people thought it was better, just as now some people think it's worse. But I think it's just part of all the magic that's out there," said Ms. Starr.

"I think Elliott and I can be normal," Nory argued.

"But what's *normal*?" Ms. Starr asked. "It was only a century ago that people separated the powers into the five Fs, you know. It's a very limited point of view. I believe there's no such thing as normal, and that we all deserve respect, just as we are."

All that was very nice, but Nory wanted to go home to her family. "Please let us try," she pleaded again.

Ms. Starr sighed. "You want to test out of my class?"

"Yes," said Nory.

Elliott nodded.

"All right," Ms. Starr said at last. "If it means that much to you, I'll ask Principal Gonzalez to evaluate you."

Nory grinned wide.

This time would be different from the Big Test.

This time she would pass.

13

Nory and Elliott practiced that afternoon at Nory's house. Aunt Margo gave them cinnamon toast for a snack, but she wasn't happy about their plan to get out of UDM.

"Oh, please," she said, sinking into a chair at the kitchen table after they explained it all to her. "Just be who you are, not who you think you should be."

Nory hated the expression on her aunt's face, but it didn't change her mind. "We'll be outside practicing," she said. "Come on, Elliott. You can bring your toast with you."

Aunt Margo's yard was full of vegetable plants and flowers. There was a line of laundry hanging out to dry in the September sun, and a small metal table with some chairs. Nory and Elliott ate and talked.

"Once we get switched to the regular classes, we'll get trained in all the regular things," Nory explained. "Did you know they don't have to do headstands? Or interpretive dance. Or group trust exercises." She told Elliott what she'd seen when she'd peeked into other classrooms: about the Flares' marshmallow lessons and the earlybird Flyers in the circle and the Fluxers working on colored kittens.

"So they were working on actual skills?" he asked. "Practical skills?"

"And we will, too," Nory said. "As soon as we get out of UDM."

"How do those other teachers teach magic?" asked Elliott. "If they don't do headstands and all that."

"They teach magic like Ms. Starr teaches math. They explain how it's done and then the students practice doing it." She slipped a hair band off her wrist and pulled her hair into a ponytail. "My father always said that good magic is like a well-trained house pet. Nobody likes a dog that barks all the time, or a cat that scratches the furniture, right?"

"I guess not."

"So people train their dogs and cats not to do that. That's how it's supposed to be with magic, too."

"Magic is like a house pet?"

"Father says you have to discipline it. The key to strong magic is to never get emotional. Stay in control. Like a dog trainer."

"Yeah, but Ms. Starr wants us to *feel* our feelings," Elliott pointed out. "And she wants us to understand our magic, not control it."

"I know," Nory said. "But I don't think she's right. Father says magic is supposed to be kept in a crate. Just like you'd do with a puppy you want to train. And when you let the puppy out, you keep it on a leash, right?"

"Yeah," Elliott said.

"But I don't think Ms. Starr believes in crates or leashes," Nory said. "And that's a problem."

"If magic is a puppy," said Elliott slowly, "Ms. Starr wants us to *love* the puppy instead of being its master."

"Yes," said Nory. "She wants us to *understand* the puppy and *connect* with the puppy, so we don't need a crate or a leash."

"But that won't work for our magic," Elliott pointed out. "If you and I want to be normal, we have to think like your father and control it, don't we?" He furrowed his brow. "I have to squash down the freeze power and only do flare."

"And I have to squash down the different animals," said Nory, "and just do regular ones."

"Yeah."

For a moment, they were silent. Nory pulled a pencil out of her backpack. "Okay, so let's think about control. Say you want to light this pencil on fire without freezing it afterward. How can you turn off your freezing and only do fire? Can you banish the freezing part of yourself?"

"Maybe?"

"What if you told the freezing part that it's a bad puppy? Tell it that it's a bad, bad puppy, and if it comes out of its crate, it'll get in big trouble. Try!"

Elliott took a breath. He stared hard at the pencil. It flared briefly, then went out.

"It didn't freeze!" yelled Nory. "It didn't freeze!"

"But it went out," said Elliott glumly. "I need it to stay lit."

"It's progress!" exclaimed Nory. "The bad puppy idea worked!"

"Okay, your turn."

Nory worked on black kitten. *Kitten, kitten, only kitten*, she thought. *No beaver, no dragon, no anything. That part of my magic is like a bad puppy. A very naughty puppy that has to stay in its crate.*

Her vision blurred and there she was. A kitten. A lovely kitten, perfectly shaped—until—

Oh drat.

Nory felt her body change. Her head grew big. Her tail grew thick. She had her kitten body, but she had the head and tail of—a goat. A small goat. But definitely a goat. She was a koat!

"Nory!" Elliott shouted. "Change back! Start over!"

I really should, Girl-Nory thought. *I should change back and start over and—*

But oooh, first I will just eat those vegetable plants, Koat-Nory interrupted. *Yes. Yum, yum, tomato plants! Yum, yum, squash plant. And what's that? Laundry on the clothesline? Yum, yum! Socks!* Koat-Nory didn't understand socks, but she was happy to fill her koat tummy with them.

"Nory! Stop! Can you even hear me?" Elliott was yelling.

Delicious socks. I wonder if there are shoes around? Koat-Nory thought. *Ooh, look, flowers! Those might be good to eat, too.* She opened her mouth to eat some flowers—only to see them freeze solid.

Ugh.

Cold!

The shock of the frozen flower in her mouth made her turn back into Girl-Nory.

"Oh, Elliott!" she wailed. "Why can't I do it? Why can't I get something right just once?"

"You're not the only one who messed up," Elliott said. "I meant to freeze a single flower, just to make you stop. But look. I froze them all. As soon as I got scared, I lost control and ruined everything."

Nory looked at Margo's flowers—or what used to be her flowers. They were all flower-shaped icicles now.

And the vegetables were eaten. And the socks.

Nory sighed. "We need a lot more practice," she said.

"And your aunt," Elliott noted glumly, "needs new rosebushes."

14

The next day passed with math, geography, poetry, group trust exercises, and interpretive dance. They also had music and gym. Everyone but Sebastian enjoyed music. When they were invited to experiment with various instruments like flutes and violins, Sebastian covered his eyes and screamed. "Are you people trying to blind me? Do you know what the sound waves on badly played musical instruments look like? Sharp! They're like knives to the eyeballs!" He had to go sit in the hall.

Gym was also a risky endeavor. Marigold shrank

two basketballs, and Elliott froze one. Bax turned into a rock when Willa passed him the ball.

Back in Ms. Starr's class, they practiced the headstands again. Lots and lots of headstands.

This time, Bax tried lying over a chair with his head upside down instead of doing the headstand. He remained human for most of the session, which made Ms. Starr very happy. Pepper was finally able to go upside down in the center of the room, not against the wall. Marigold's headstand was good, but she hit her leg on the hot radiator when she came down. There was a large burn across the bare skin of her ankle, and she held on to it, crying.

"Let me help," said Elliott. He grabbed an eraser from a nearby desk and froze it solid. Then he handed it to Marigold.

She pressed it to the burn. "Wow," she said, looking at him as if he were a hero. "Thanks."

"Don't mention it," Elliott told her. "As in, really. Please don't talk about it outside this classroom."

When the school bell rang at three o'clock, Ms.

Starr called Nory and Elliott to her desk. "Here," she said, handing them each a piece of paper. Her voice sagged a bit, Nory thought.

Your evaluation is approved, the papers read. *Your test will be a week from Friday. Come to the gymnasium thirty minutes before school starts—and remember: Luck comes in many different forms.* It was signed by Principal Gonzalez.

That afternoon, they practiced at Elliott's house.

Mr. Cohen had big hair like Elliott. He worked from home as a guitar teacher. He was a Flicker, and from what Nory could tell, he mainly used his talent to make Elliott's baby brother laugh by making toys disappear and reappear.

"Nory, Elliott's told us about your magic. Sounds like you're a real dynamo." Mr. Cohen grinned. "You sprayed those Sparkie kids, huh? Give me five!"

Nory smiled shyly and touched her palm to his. Her heart both stretched and shrank. Why couldn't her own father high-five her magic?

"We're going to my room, Dad," Elliott said. "We have homework."

"Let me show Nory your ices first," Mr. Cohen said, explaining to Nory, "I keep a photo album. I take pictures of as many as I can."

"She doesn't care, Dad," Elliott said. "Nobody cares." He pulled Nory past his father and upstairs. "I've asked him to stop taking pictures of every little freeze, but he won't." He raised his voice. "Obviously he hates me, or he wouldn't try to embarrass me every minute of my life."

From downstairs, Elliott's dad laughed. "I *adore* you, kiddo!" he called. "And come on, the frozen TV remote was cool!"

"No, it was just frozen," Elliott grumbled. "Which meant it was broken."

He and Nory settled on the floor in his room. Elliott lined up a row of candles to practice on, and also a row of Popsicle sticks.

Then they got to work.

It did not go well.

Elliott froze one candle after another.

Nory turned into another koat and ate the candles.

Elliott froze some Popsicle sticks.

Nory turned into a dritten and blew fire at Elliott's bedspread.

Elliott froze the bedspread and put the fire out, leaving an icy scorch mark in its place.

Nory turned back into a human. She groaned and put her head in her hands.

"It was an ugly bedspread anyway," Elliott said.

They both laughed, but they knew they were in trouble.

At school the next morning, Nory opened her desk and found a book inside: *The Box of Normal* by Eugenia Throckmorton.

Who had put it there? Ms. Starr?

Unlikely. *Normal* was one of her least favorite words.

But no one else knew that Nory and Elliott were trying to switch classes. They had decided not to discuss it with the others. They didn't want their classmates to feel bad.

Nory flipped through the thin, crinkly pages. She gobbled up the words.

Elliott arrived and slid into his seat just as Ms. Starr called the class to attention. Nory hid her book in her lap and kept reading.

The person with upside-down abilities who wishes to pass as normal should use a technique I call "the box of normal," Eugenia Throckmorton had written.

The book explained that there was a history of Flares, like Elliott, who were Freezers as well. Very often the freezing overwhelmed the flare talent. The book also gave examples of unusual Fluxers. In one case there was a boy who shifted into large carnivores from the day he turned ten. When he was fifteen, he was doing extinct animals: velociraptors and tyrannosaurs. Luckily, the "box of normal" skill helped him limit himself to bears. In another case, a girl suffered from turning into insect after insect, never by choice. She had once been trapped as a fly for a whole week. Yet again, the "box of normal" helped. Using that skill, the girl learned to turn herself into a ladybug—and to switch back to a girl at any time.

Nory couldn't find anything about Fluxers like Bax, who turned into objects.

It didn't mention Fierces, either, or people who shrank things or made indoor rainstorms.

Then there was a long and probably boring section on licensing and legal stuff, so Nory jumped ahead to the instructions.

Throckmorton wrote that to do normal magic you should "box in" the tiny regular part of your wonky talent. *The rest of your talent is an unruly jungle*, she wrote. *Deep inside the jungle, you build a safe place to go. The safe place is the box, your box of normal.*

Nory thought her box of normal was the black kitten. She could hold black kitten longer than she could hold any other form. She had a normal skunk, too. She could do that for a little while, at least.

Elliott's box of normal was the way he could heat marshmallows and light matches.

Maybe there was a box of normal for Andres, too. He *could* fly. He just couldn't come down.

But was there a box of normal for people like Bax, Pepper, Marigold, and Willa?

Nory worried that there wasn't. The thought made her sad. But not so sad that she stopped reading.

By lunchtime, Nory felt like a changed person.

"Come with me *now*," she said to Elliott. They didn't go to the cafeteria. Instead, they hid in the supply closet. "We've been going about it all wrong!" she explained.

"We have?" Elliott said.

"Yes, but now I know what to do." Nory explained about Throckmorton's book and the box of normal. "I've been building my box of normal all morning, and I want to see if it works. I'm going to do kitten, okay?"

"I don't want to be in a small space with you when you flux," said Elliott.

"Please?"

"You might burn me with dragon fire."

"You'll be fine. You have ice power!"

"You might skunk spray me or chew my shoes."

"Elliott! Please. This could help us both!"

Elliott rolled his eyes. "Okay, fine. But if anything goes upside down, I'm going to leave the closet and lock you inside."

"Nothing's going to go upside down, and you want to know why?" Nory grinned. "Because I've got a box of normal!"

"Huh?"

"I've been building a safe place inside my brain all morning."

She closed her eyes. In her mind, she saw a box, and inside the box was the part of her magic that let her make ordinary animals. Ordinary animals with human minds.

It was a small box. A tiny box, really. The jungle of her magic was enormous, it seemed.

No matter. She was safe inside her tiny box. Safe and sound and *kitten, kitten, kitten* . . .

Her vision blurred and her body shifted.

Kitten!

"You did it!" Elliott exclaimed. "Now just stay that way, okay? No funny business." He reached down and patted her kitten head. "You look awesome. Nice job on the fluffy ears, and you have good long whiskers."

Kitten-Nory purred. She knew that the boy who was petting her was Elliott. She knew they were friends. She understood what he was saying. Box of normal!

Kitten-Nory walked around the supply closet in the dim light. She thought about her regular Nory life. She stayed completely kitten-shaped.

Then, because she decided to, she popped back into her own Nory body. She looked at Elliott with wonder.

"That was great!" Elliott said. "Oh my gosh. Nory! I timed it on my phone, and you were a kitten for a whole ten minutes!"

"I did it," Nory said. She felt tired and proud. "And if I can, you can, too."

At the end of the day, Nory pushed through the crowded hall to drink from the water fountain. It was invisible again, but by now she knew where it was. When she finished, she looked up to see Pepper beside her.

"So?" Pepper asked. It was the first time she'd looked Nory in the eye since the skunkephant in the cafeteria.

"So what?"

"So how's it going? With Elliott, and practicing for your test. Are you getting closer?"

"You know we're trying to switch out of UDM?"

"Yeah. I heard you guys talking about it."

"Does everyone know?"

"I don't think so."

Nory's mind felt dull. Then the pieces of the puzzle came together. "The book. Did *you* leave it for me?"

"Well." Pepper shrugged. "I thought it might work for you and Elliott. It definitely doesn't work for me. I've got no normal to put in the box."

Nory looked at Pepper and saw the small, friendly girl she'd first met—the girl Pepper was to her before Nory knew she was a Fierce.

Nory had liked that girl. A lot.

Poor Pepper, Nory thought. *How lonely she must be. How awful to have a talent that pushes people away.*

"It *is* working," Nory said. "The box and all that, it's made a huge difference. Thank you."

"You're welcome," Pepper said wistfully. "I don't fit in anywhere. I don't think I ever will. But maybe you can."

15

The box of normal worked for Elliott, too. He tried it that afternoon at his house, with Nory looking on. He lit a candle. He lit two candles. He lit three.

"Elliott!" Nory said. "Three candles and no freezing. That was awesome!"

Elliott was clearly pleased. He blew the candles out with a poof of air.

He roasted a marshmallow perfectly, too.

"Mmm," said Nory, taking a bite. "Delicious. Do you want some?"

He shook his head. "I don't like marshmallows."

"Really? What's not to love?" Nory popped the rest of it in her mouth.

Elliott shrugged. "I'm more into ice cream. Go ahead and laugh. A Freezer who likes ice cream, haw. I've heard it before."

"I wasn't going to laugh."

"Lacey thinks it's *hilarious*."

"Oh, come on. Everybody likes ice cream. That's why it's great to be a Freezer. Maybe one day you'll be able to make it with just your hands!"

Elliott shook his head. "No, I won't. Remember? If the box of normal keeps working, I won't freeze anything ever again."

Nory was silent for a minute. What Elliott had just said seemed kind of sad. But then again, he didn't want to be a Freezer. He wanted to be a Flare. "No problem," she told him, brightly. "Who needs to make ice cream? You can always buy it at the store."

• • •

The next week, they practiced every chance they got. Day after day.

Nory became a puppy. The puppy did *not* sprout squid legs.

Nory became a skunk. The skunk did not grow an elephant trunk.

Elliott cooked eggs and marshmallows. Sometimes they were burnt or undercooked, but never ever did they freeze.

Andres was the second person to notice something was up, or at least the second person to say something out loud about it.

It happened Wednesday morning. They were doing a trust activity.

First, everyone had to choose a partner. Nory chose Elliott.

Then Ms. Starr gave each pair of students a large mixing bowl full of whipped cream. Hidden within the cream, she explained, were cherries. The same number in each bowl: more than five, fewer than twenty-five.

"The team who finds the most cherries wins," Ms. Starr said. Her eyes danced. "But, there's a catch."

"Of course there is," Bax grumbled. He'd been paired with Andres for a partner, which required him to grab Andres's leash and haul him down from the ceiling, hand over hand. Then he handed Andres the bag of bricks. Even so, Andres still floated a foot off the floor, like a boy-shaped balloon.

"What's the catch?" Willa asked. Her partner was Pepper, and Nory noticed that they were wearing striped shirts. These days, they often coordinated clothes.

"The catch is that you have to find the cherries using only your mouths!" Ms. Starr bounced on her toes. "Just your mouths. Not your hands."

Everyone looked at her.

"Um, what about germs?" Marigold said.

"No one's sick, are they?" Ms. Starr asked. She barreled on. "Great, then."

"I am going to have problems with this," Sebastian said. "The sound waves of slurping are absurdly bright. I will need sunglasses."

"You can close your eyes," said Ms. Starr.

"How does this exercise build trust?" Elliott asked.

"You get whipped cream all over your faces," the teacher answered. "It's going to be hilarious! You'll laugh with each other, not *at* each other, which builds community. But it's also an exercise meant to stretch your brains. This is not the typical way to find cherries. It'll develop your natural instincts!"

"*Is* there a typical way to find cherries?" Elliott asked.

"Yeah. It's called the grocery store," Willa said.

"My natural instinct is to not stick my face into a bowl of whipped cream," Bax said.

Ms. Starr ignored him. She raised her chin and said, "Ready, set . . . go!"

Sebastian dove into the whipped cream. He emerged with a fluffy white beard, thick white eyebrows, and closed eyes. He licked the whipped cream off his mouth. "Yummy. Have I got any on my face?"

Marigold had put her face into a bowl, too. "I did it!" she cried. She had wide, round eyes within peaks of white. She moved her mouth around and spit a red cherry into her hand. "Yay, me!"

It was fun. Everyone began bobbing in and out of the bowls. Willa used the whipped cream to spike up her bangs. Pepper dipped only her nose into the whipped cream. Then she lifted her head with what looked like a glob of white snot.

"Kleenex?" she deadpanned.

Andres choked on a cherry, and Bax hit him on the back, causing a blob of cream to splatter all over Bax's shirt. Everyone laughed. Even Bax.

Nory sat back. She soaked in the chaos and grinned. It was undeniably fun.

Then she remembered: "Fun" wouldn't get her and Elliott out of the UDM class and into regular classes. They needed to use this time to focus on the box of normal.

Nory fished around in the bowl of cream with her hand and pulled out a cherry, which she cleaned off with her shirt. She held the cherry out to Elliott. "Light the stem on fire."

Elliott lifted his eyebrows. "I can try, I guess." He glanced around. "But there's a lot going on."

"That's the point," Nory said. "You know, in the book. You have to be able to ignore distraction."

Elliott concentrated. *Poof!* The cherry stem burst into flame.

"Nice!" Nory said, quickly dropping the cherry back into the wet bowl of cream. She pulled out a new cherry with her hand. "This time, light just the tip. Like a candle."

Elliott squinted and a tiny flame flared on the tippity tip of the stem.

"Elliott! Yes!" Nory cried.

"Hey," Andres accused. "No fair." He set down

his bag of bricks and drifted up to the ceiling, and his voice boomed louder. "Nory's using her hands to get the cherries out—and Elliott's lighting them on fire!"

Everyone stopped what they were doing. Their whipped-cream-covered faces swiveled in Nory and Elliott's direction.

"You're doing your magic the right way," Willa said in a funny voice. "How'd you learn to light things on fire instead of freezing them?"

Nory gulped. She sensed Elliott stiffening beside her.

"Nory and Elliott," Ms. Starr said quietly, "I would appreciate if you could focus on *my* exercise while you're in *my* classroom."

"What does she mean?" Willa asked. "What other classroom would you be in?"

Nory couldn't tell everyone what she and Elliott were doing. She couldn't say to their faces that she wanted out of their class. "It was the germs!" she exclaimed. "Like Marigold said earlier!"

Marigold looked confused.

"I got grossed out," Nory insisted. "That's why Elliott lit the cherry on fire. Because I'm afraid of germs."

She wasn't a fan of germs, but after growing up in a house with twelve rabbits and a toucan, she wasn't actually afraid of them. Not as afraid as she was about staying here, in the Upside-Down Magic class.

Pepper cleared her throat. "People have trouble following rules when they get scared. I'm afraid of snakes," she offered.

Nory shot her a grateful look.

"I'm afraid of worms," Willa said. "And they come out when it rains."

"Ah, so this is turning out to be a trust exercise of a different kind," Ms. Starr said. She clasped her hands. "In fact, this is a teachable moment."

Everyone groaned.

"Let's each share something we're scared of," Ms. Starr said, passing out individually wrapped wipes. "Nory is scared of germs, Pepper's scared of worms—"

"Snakes," Pepper corrected.

"*I'm* worms," Willa said.

"And I'm scared of heights," Ms. Starr finished. "It's silly! I know! But there it is. Andres? What are you scared of?"

"Wide-open spaces," he said.

Everyone nodded, and just like that, the others jumped in. Elliott was scared of clowns; Sebastian was afraid of thunderstorms and rock concerts. Marigold was scared of having foods touch each other on her plate. "I absolutely *detest* gravy," she said with a shiver. "Gravy creeps me out because it mushes everything together."

"Yes, I suppose it does," Ms. Starr said. She turned to Bax, the only student who hadn't gone. "Bax? Would you like to share?"

"No, thanks," Bax said.

"Would you share anyway, please?"

Bax glowered at Nory as if this new trust exercise was all her fault.

No one spoke.

The silence grew uncomfortable.

Finally, Bax mumbled something that Nory couldn't make out.

"I'm sorry, what?" Ms. Starr said.

"Sllldgmrrrs," Bax said, staring at the carpet.

"One more time?"

Bax exhaled. "*Sledgehammers*. All right?"

"Sledgehammers?" Willa said. "Why?"

"I get it," Elliott said. "Because of the rock thing."

"*Ohhh*," the others said.

"It's a stupid thing to be afraid of," Bax muttered.

"No, it's not," Elliott said. "I wouldn't want a sledge-hammer hitting me. I wouldn't even want a *very small* hammer hitting me!"

He said it so earnestly that everyone laughed.

"I'm not kidding," he insisted. "Hammers of all kinds are serious."

Bax didn't smile at Elliott, but he didn't scowl, either.

Nory felt a rush of affection for Elliott, who was kind to people on purpose. She felt a rush of affection for Bax, too. It surprised her.

But I still want out, she told herself. *Anyway, being moved to a regular class doesn't mean I can't be friends with the UDM kids.*

Bax gave Elliott an awkward fist bump.

Nory looked away. When everyone went around sharing their fears, she was the only one who hadn't told the truth.

Finally it was Friday, the day of the test. Nory and Elliott arrived early to school. A woman wearing a narrow skirt and holding a clipboard waited for them outside the gymnasium. "Elliott Cohen?" she asked.

"Yes?" Elliott squeaked.

"Go on, then," the woman said, pushing open the door to the gym.

"Good luck! You'll be great! Toast it to perfection!" Nory called.

Elliott looked back at Nory. His eyes were wide. The woman with the clipboard followed behind and the door swung shut.

Nory paced. She tried to crack her knuckles. She did jumping jacks to help get her anxiety out. It felt like forever.

Finally, Elliott burst through the gymnasium doors, beaming from ear to ear.

"Perfect marshmallow!" he shouted. "Principal Gonzalez even ate it—he popped it right into his mouth—and said it was the best marshmallow he'd had all day! I mean, I know it was the only marshmallow he'd had all day, but who cares?"

Nory jumped up and down. "Zamboozle! I am so proud of you!"

The woman with the clipboard cleared her throat. "Elinor Horace?" She let Nory into the gym.

"You're going to ace it," Elliott called out after her. "Box of normal for the win!"

The door shut solidly behind her. She flinched. The gym didn't have as much of an echo when she came in with the rest of her class. It was the same room with the scarred wooden floor she'd been in many times before, but it felt different now. Bigger. Scarier.

Principal Gonzalez was nowhere in sight, but Nory wasn't surprised. Elliott had told her on the first day that the principal was invisible.

"Come in, come in," a voice boomed. Nory turned toward the sound, and now there was a man sitting in the middle row of the rickety gym bleachers. A tall man, with a big silly mustache, tan skin, no hair, and a three-piece velvet suit.

Then he was gone.

Then he was there.

Then he settled into being halfway visible and a pale shade of blue, which Nory knew was quite a difficult Flicker trick.

"So you're Stone Horace's daughter," the man said. "We went to Sage Academy together, did you know that? Went through all our Flicker studies side by side."

"You're friends with Father?"

"No," he said with a sigh. "Not friends. Competitors, you might say. And we have very different educational ideals. But he's a smart, smart man." For a second, the principal seemed lost in thought. Then he pulled himself back. "You go by Nory?"

Nory nodded.

He stood and extended his hand. "Principal Gonzalez. Very pleased to meet you."

"Pleased to meet you, too," Nory said, shaking his hand. It was solid, even though he looked only partly there.

"I am quite excited about this year's Upside-Down Magic class," the principal continued. "I'm sorry to hear you want to leave. I don't know for *sure* that it's the best way to teach students with different magics, but I sure hope this will be a good solution. You know, teachers have been arguing about Upside-Down Magic education for a long time. There are many different theories. Now, many UDM classes are starting up around the country. I have high hopes they'll make a positive change."

"Ms. Starr is a really good teacher," Nory said. It was true. Saying it made Nory realize it for sure.

"But you still want to leave?"

She nodded.

"It's a pity," he said. "But if it really matters to you, let's give you a chance." The principal sat back down on the bleachers and slapped his hands on his thighs. "Let's see your kitten, shall we? All black, if you please."

Nory concentrated on her box of normal. She stayed within its safe walls and did her kitten.

She did it perfectly. She held still as Principal Gonzalez inspected her whiskers and teeth, tail and ear fluff. She meowed and followed instructions to jump up on a chair and roll over.

The woman in the narrow skirt opened a can of tuna fish and set it on the floor. Nory didn't eat it.

Then the woman changed into a mouse and ran in front of Nory. Nory's human mind stayed in control.

She didn't chase the mouse.

Then the woman changed into a butterfly and flew around her head.

Nory didn't chase that, either.

"Fine work, fine work indeed," Principal Gonzalez said. "You may return to human form, now, please."

Nory popped from cat to girl.

"All right, then," Principal Gonzalez said. "You've done very well, you and Elliott both."

"Can we switch to the normal magic classes, then?" Nory asked.

"There are other factors to think about," the principal said. "But you should be very proud of yourselves." He studied her, stroking his chin. "I'll have an answer for you by the end of the day."

Elliott waited outside the gym for Nory. The bell rang to start the day and they ran all the way to class.

"Never, never again!" Elliott practically sang. "Never again will I freeze a flower or turn a pizza into a disc of ice. My freezing days are over!"

"And no more skunkephants for me," Nory said. To her surprise, she felt a pang of loss. She pushed it away.

Elliott stopped running. His cheeks were rosy. "Nory? We're *normal*."

Nory nodded. "As long as we stay in our boxes."

16

The UDM students, Nory and Elliott among them, did math and geography and expressed their feelings through interpretive dance. They did headstands.

Bax went to the nurse.

"My eyes, my eyes!" Sebastian cried during music class. He shielded them with his hands. "If you have to sing, can't you at least sing on key?"

"If you have to complain, can't you at least do it in your head?" Andres called from the ceiling.

Sebastian looked up and stuck out his tongue. Andres grinned. Nory suppressed a smile. There might be *some* things she'd miss once she got transferred out of the UDM class.

Later in the morning, Ms. Starr guided them through a "centering" activity. The students were supposed to balance on their right legs and lean forward, their arms outstretched like wings.

"Yes, Willa!" she said. "Now straighten your left leg and s-t-r-e-t-c-h your left foot behind you. Oh dear, Elliott? Are you all right?"

Elliott was not very centered. He toppled over time after time. At first he laughed, but as the rest of the class got better and he didn't, Nory could see that it bothered him.

"Don't worry about it," she told him, hopping over on her right leg. She was *about* to say, "We won't have to do centering exercises when we get to the regular class," but Bax spoke over her. "Dude. Pinch your earlobe."

"Huh?" Elliott said.

"When you wobble, pinch your right earlobe."

Elliott planted his right leg. He stretched out his arms and leaned forward. He extended his left leg behind him and wobbled like crazy.

"Whoa," he said, pinwheeling his arms.

"Grab your earlobe! Pinch it!" Bax said.

Elliott did, and he found his balance. Then he stretched his arm out again.

He was a perfect airplane. He beamed.

"How'd you know the earlobe thing?" he asked Bax.

"I'm a rock half the time. Rocks don't wobble."

"Rocks don't have earlobes, either," Elliott said. He frowned.

"Fine," Bax said. "My mom makes me go to yoga class with her."

"Well, thanks," Elliott said. He came out of his airplane and bumped knuckles with Bax again. They did that almost every day now.

Nory wondered if there were things Elliott might miss about UDM, too.

She decided not to ask.

• • •

After lunch, Ms. Starr's class joined the other kids for recess in the yard. As usual, the UDM kids hung out by the swing set. Today, Elliott brought up the rear, holding Andres on his leash. He barely stopped at the swings, however, and handed the leash to Nory. "Got to go," he said. "The Sparkies will want to hear the good news!"

"Elliott, wait!" Nory said. She stepped apart from the others and lowered her voice. Andres was float-ing a safe distance away. "Principal Gonzalez hasn't told us officially yet."

"Yeah, but come on. We aced it."

Nory bit her finger. "Still. Why do you want to tell the Sparkies?"

"They'll be excited for me," Elliott said. "You'll see. We've been friends forever and they're awesome. They just weren't comfortable with the freezing, which is really understandable."

He dashed down the hill toward Zinnia, Lacey,

and Rune, who were clustered by the woody area near the yard boundary.

"What does he see in those guys?" Nory asked, back at the swing set.

Marigold wrinkled her nose. "I think they're mean."

Something twitched against Nory's wrist. It was Andres's leash, pulling roughly against her skin.

"Something's going wrong with Elliott and the Sparkies," he called down. "We should go over there."

"What's happening?" Nory asked. She couldn't see the woodsy area, but Andres was up high enough to see it. He frog-kicked his legs, making Nory stumble. "Nory! Let's go. Those guys are being jerks!"

Nory and the other UDM kids took off at a sprint. Nory pulled Andres along. They found Elliott just past the tree line, where it was hard for the lunch ladies to see. He was with the Sparkies in a shadowy spot between two oaks. They had him backed up against a tree.

Lacey held a stick that was on fire.

"Come on, just one for each of us," Zinnia was saying.

"You don't understand," Elliott said. "I'm normal now."

"But we *weally* want Popsicles," Lacey said in a baby voice. "If you were *weally* our *fwiend*, you'd make us some." She waved the flaming stick at Elliott's head.

"He can't make Popsicles out of thin air," Andres called from up high. "Leave him alone!"

The Sparkies swiveled their heads and peered at the sky.

"Or what?" Lacey challenged. "You'll spit on me?" Zinnia laughed.

"Seriously," said Bax. "Elliott, come over here with us." Elliott hesitated for a second but then came to stand with the UDM kids. "Don't mess with him again," Bax said to the Sparkies.

"Oooh, I'm scared!" said Lacey. "Big bad Bax might turn into a rock!"

Bax snarled. "If I do, I hope I land on your foot."

"Now, Lacey, don't be mean," Zinnia said. "Bax can't help it that he's always turning into a rock. He's just *wonky*." She swept her hand in an arc. "They all are."

"We are not wonky," said Willa. "We're *different*."

"No one says *wonky* anymore," added Marigold. "It's so old-fashioned. You sound like my grandmother."

"Changing the label doesn't change the facts," said Lacey. "Ask anyone. You guys are as wonky as, oh, as wonky as a skunk with an elephant trunk. Ooh, that rhymes!" She laughed. "Wonky as a skunk with an elephant trunk!"

"Don't," Nory snapped.

Lacey smirked. "Wow. Great comeback."

"Stop it."

"That's all you've got to say?" Lacey retorted. She walked toward Nory. "It blows my mind that your father is headmaster of Sage Academy, while you're just *you*. Wonky, weird, and oh so smelly."

Andres muttered under his breath. Then he hocked up a huge loogie and *ptthht!* A mouthful landed smack on Lacey's head. It snaked down her forehead and oozed behind her glasses.

"Ew," said Zinnia. "Lacey, that is super gross."

Rune laughed.

Lacey screwed her mouth into an ugly shape and flung her hand in Andres's direction. There was a spark, and Andres's leash started to smolder. Tiny tongues of flame shot out. Nory screamed.

"Andres's leash is on fire!" she cried. "You guys! Help!"

Andres yelled in fright. The flames reached higher.

Willa frowned and pressed her fingers to her temples. Nothing happened. "I don't rain outdoors yet!" she wailed.

Sebastian stood helpless.

Marigold, too. "I'd shrink his leash," she said, worrying her hands. "But what if that makes his clothes catch fire?"

The leash was burning away. Now only threads

kept Andres from ballooning into space. The heat reached Nory's hand, but she held tight.

"Help!" Andres cried. "If the leash breaks, I'll keep going up forever!"

"I'll get a Flyer from up in the yard," Marigold said.

Sebastian grabbed her arm. "Won't help. The only kids out here are fifth graders—"

"And they can only fly two feet up," Marigold finished. "And the lunch ladies! They're all Fuzzies!"

Nory's breaths came fast. She shot Elliott a desperate look, because she knew what needed to be done, and so did he.

"You have to help," she told him. "Come on. You can do it."

He hesitated.

"You have to! Forget the stupid box of normal! Andres needs help!"

Elliott pressed his lips together. He flung his fingers out with intense determination.

The leash froze from top to bottom.

With a hiss, the fire was gone.

"Elliott!" Nory cried triumphantly. "Yes!"

Andres's body sagged with relief.

"You're okay. We'll get you down," Nory called. Hand over hand, she started pulling the frozen leash toward her.

"You saved him!" Marigold said to Elliott.

"I did!" Elliott said.

But he hadn't.

With a terrifying sound, the frozen leash creaked. Splinters of ice rained down.

C-r-r-r-a-ck.

It snapped in two.

"Nooooooo!" Nory cried.

Andres went up, his arms and legs flailing.

Super fast.

Super high.

Lacey laughed.

Everyone else jabbered, throwing out panicked suggestions.

"Knock him down with pinecones!"

"Throw a net over him!"

"Get an advanced Flyer—quick!"

Sebastian sprinted back to the school to get a teacher, but Andres was already high above the tree-tops. By the time a Flyer arrived on the scene, Andres would be gone.

Nory dug her fingernails into her palms. Andres was going up and up and up. Before long, no one would be able to save him.

Unless . . .

Nory sucked in breath. First she imagined her box of normal. Next, she imagined the walls of the box exploding outward in all directions.

No more box.

No more normal.

Then she pictured a bird, big and fast and strong. She had never done bird—never, not ever—and so many things could go wrong. But she concentrated with all her might, imagining wings and talons and eyes with perfect vision.

"Nory! Yes!" Elliott said.

Bird-Nory looked down to see Elliott jumping and clapping.

"Go, Nory!" Marigold urged. "Hurry!"

Bird-Nory swooped through the sky. *Maybe I should go build a nest.*

No nest! Girl-Nory commanded. *Andres. Only Andres.*

Bird-Nory spotted him, a lumpish thing in a stripy shirt, flying into the sky without any feathers.

Nah, thought Bird-Nory, swerving away. *I'd rather search for worms.*

He doesn't have feathers, but he's still your friend, Girl-Nory told her bird self, and Bird-Nory heard and listened.

Bird-Nory flew to the lumpish thing. She looked him straight in the eye.

Wow, he was huge.

She must be small.

Bird-Nory craned her neck to catch a glimpse of herself. *Oh, drat,* Girl-Nory thought. *A bluebird? Seriously?*

She had to grow, that was all there was to it.

Grow! Girl-Nory told herself. *Go on, now! GROW!*

She quivered.

She strained.

Nothing. She was still a tiny bluebird, with big Andres floating higher and higher beside her.

But why wouldn't she grow? Was Nory's stupid wonky magic so wonky that she couldn't even wonk it when she wanted to?

Ms. Starr's words came into Nory's head: *We should nurture what's inside us.*

Well, there was a lot of different magic inside Nory. That was for sure. When she drew her box of normal, it was teeny-tiny compared to the part of herself she had to leave out. And in the part of her she had to leave out, there was definitely magic that could make her grow. She knew it because of the skunkephant.

I'm nurturing you, inner skunkephant! she thought. She nurtured it as hard as she could. *Come on already!*

No luck.

In her mind, she heard Ms. Starr's voice again.

UDM isn't about controlling your feelings, it's about understanding them.

Okay, she'd try that. What was she feeling?

Worry, for Andres. Disgust, at Lacey.

Annoyance at Elliott for trying to be friends with Lacey. Sympathy with him, for wanting friends.

Hope that she and Pepper could one day be friends.

Anger at Father. Frustration with Dalia and Hawthorn. Missing them, too.

Pride at doing a good bluebird, but fear of what people might say if she turned her bluebird into something else.

Those were her feelings. The feelings of Nory Boxwood Horace, right then, as she fluttered in front of Andres in the sky.

And that did it. Nory grew—and grew and grew and grew. She was Enormous-Bluebird-Nory.

"Aaaaaaah!" Andres screamed. He kicked, trying to get away.

Enormous-Bluebird-Nory changed again. Her bird-face shifted. She recognized the stretchiness of her skin and the flutter of her eyelashes. Now she had her girl face. *Whoa.*

Nory had never heard of a Fluxer who could do part animal and part human.

"Andres, it's me, Nory," said Enormous-Bluebird-Nory-with-Nory's-Actual-Face.

Andres's eyes bugged.

"It is. Really. I'm going to save you now, okay?"

Enormous-Bluebird-Nory-with-Nory's-Actual-Face grabbed hold of Andres with her claw feet. He was heavy, and the pull of his upside-down magic was strong, but she flapped her powerful wings and delivered him safely to the ground.

Everyone from UDM cheered.

Nory, relieved and exhausted, turned back into herself.

And Andres, no longer in the clutches of a giant bird, started floating back up again.

No!

Nory grabbed his ankle.

But the more anxious Andres was, the stronger his magic became.

He kept going up.

Elliott grabbed Nory's leg, and that helped. But Andres's floating magic was strong, and soon Elliott was lifted off the ground as well.

Willa grabbed Elliott. "We need a rope! Somebody find a rope!"

Zinnia and Rune took off toward the school, but before they were halfway there, Marigold gasped and pointed.

"There!" she said.

It was Bax.

He was a rope.

Marigold passed Rope-Bax to Elliott, who passed him to Nory, who tied him to Andres's belt. She gave a yank to make sure the knot would hold.

Rope-Bax held on to Andres.

Nory gave Rope-Bax to Willa, who wrapped the loose end around her wrist for added security.

Clumsily, everyone (except for Andres) climbed down to the ground.

They were safe. Andres was safe.

It took a minute for it to sink in.

"Thanks, Bax," Andres said to the rope.

Rope-Bax didn't answer.

"Who's Sebastian talking to?" Elliott wondered.

They turned to look. Sebastian was running over, speaking to the air.

"Sebastian!" yelled Nory. "Who are you talking to?"

Something next to Sebastian shimmered.

A shoe appeared, then a jacket. Then the rest of Principal Gonzalez's body appeared, with his mustache coming in last. With a wiggle of his lips, as if to make sure every hair was in place, he said, "He was talking to me."

17

Principal Gonzalez pulled a blue leather leash from his pocket. He walked over and fastened it onto Andres's belt and unlooped Rope-Bax. He handed the leash to Nory and Rope-Bax back to Willa.

"Take Bax to Nurse Riley. He'll know what to do." The principal paused. "I wouldn't watch, though, if I were you."

Willa hurried off. Lacey, eyes on the ground, crept behind her like a crab hoping not to be noticed.

"*Chhht,*" Principal Gonzalez said, holding up one finger. "Not so fast, Lacey Clench."

Lacey slumped. Then she turned around. She pasted on a smile and said, "I'm so glad Andres is safe. I mean, Elliott? The way he iced that leash and broke it? Upside-Down Magic is really dangerous." She blinked innocently. "Not to be mean. I'm just saying."

The principal frowned. "Let's talk about *you*, Lacey. Do you think it was clever to set fire to someone's leash?"

"No, sir. I know it was unsupervised flaring, but it was an accident. My control isn't good at all. You can ask my teacher. We used the fire extinguishers four times because of me, just last week."

Gonzalez raised his eyebrows.

"It was a mistake, I swear," continued Lacey. "I didn't Flare his leash on purpose."

"Hmm," Principal Gonzalez said. "You are lucky that the UDM class acted so quickly, and so creatively."

He regarded her. "Otherwise he might have died. Do you understand?"

Lacey's face drained of color. "Yes, sir."

"All right. Now let's talk about your manners. Would you like being mocked for your glasses, or for anything else that separates you from others?"

Lacey swallowed and shook her head.

"I did not think so."

"I have to wear them," Lacey said. "They're prescription."

"I will not tolerate bigotry," said Principal Gonzalez. "I will not tolerate unkindness about race, gender, orientation, family background, religion, weight, magical abilities, favorite candy, or anything else that distinguishes one person from another. Not here at Dunwiddle Magic School."

"It was an accident," whispered Lacey.

"Possibly what you *did* was an accident. But what you said to Elliott and his UDM classmates was most certainly a choice. We can discuss it more in my office. Zinnia and Rune are there now. Please go and join them."

When Lacey was gone, Principal Gonzalez sent the UDM class back to Ms. Starr's room.

Everyone except Nory and Elliott.

"You can guess what I've got to say, can't you?" Principal Gonzalez said to Nory and Elliott once the others were gone.

Shame clogged Nory's throat.

Then pride swelled her up.

Then shame.

Then pride.

Her different magic had been on display for everyone to see. A giant Nory-faced bluebird? She would never live it down.

But she had saved Andres!

It was horrible.

It was great!

"I think you're going to say that we did a very

good thing today," Elliott said. "And that you're glad because we saved Andres. *But* we'll have to work extra hard not to let our wonky magic take over again."

Principal Gonzalez tilted his head. "Is that truly your prediction?"

"If we study the *Box of Normal* book, we'll get better," Elliott said doggedly. "Especially, you know, since we'll be in the normal classes. Nothing like this will happen again, Mr. Gonzalez, I promise."

The principal's eyes were very dark and very kind. "Nory, Elliott—you belong in Ms. Starr's class."

"What?" Elliott said. "B-both of us?" His breath hitched. "It was just one small bit of ice, to save Andres!"

"Magic like yours needs the right kind of training," Gonzalez said. "What happened with Andres has helped me realize what I probably knew all along." He pursed his lips. "You won't get proper training in a regular Flare class, Elliott. And you won't get it in a Fluxer class, either, Nory. I don't know how you did what you did, but I am quite sure that Ms. Starr's teaching played a role. Do you agree?"

Nory nodded. Ms. Starr's teaching had definitely played a role.

Principal Gonzalez escorted them across the lawn. "That's my verdict, then. The Upside-Down Magic class is where you belong."

Elliott looked stricken. "But—"

"My decision is final," Principal Gonzalez said.

He disappeared. All at once, with a slight popping sound.

Nory and Elliott sat together on the lawn. Elliott was sulking. Nory was thinking.

She wouldn't be moving to the regular Fluxer class.

That meant she would never test again for Sage Academy. And that meant she wouldn't be going home.

Disappointment washed over her.

Could she find a bright side? She decided to compliment Elliott. At least she could help him feel better about himself.

"What you did was really important magic," she said. "Turning the leash to ice. Who else but you could have done that?"

He snorted. "No one but Elliott the Upside-Down Flare."

Nory bit her lower lip. "I have a small secret to tell you. Being an enormous bird-girl was actually kind of amazing."

"Really?"

"Really. It was. It felt *powerful*."

For a moment, Elliott showed no reaction. Then he smiled and said, "The ice magic felt pretty good, too." He plucked a piece of grass. "But the Sparkies are never going to talk to me again."

Nory made a face. "And that's a problem because . . . ?"

Elliott squinted at her. Then he laughed. The big, snorty laugh that had first made Nory like him. "I guess it's not a problem, huh?"

"*They're* the problem," Nory said.

"You're right. I should freeze their pillows."

"Or their underwear."

They laughed together.

A flash of movement caught Nory's eye. It was Marigold, running across the field. She stopped in front of them and rested her hands on her legs, breathing hard. She grinned. "Ms. Starr said to get to class, please. She got ice cream cups from the cafeteria and she's not going to make us do geography today. And Bax is back in human shape."

Elliott stood. He pulled Nory up, too. "Come on," he said.

"Are you sure?" she asked him.

Elliott nodded. "I'm sure. If there's ice cream, I'm in."

18

A week later, Elliott, Marigold, Willa, Bax, Nory, and Sebastian had a picnic in Aunt Margo's backyard. Andres floated above them, his leash tied to a table.

It was one of the last warm days of the year. They could smell the change of leaves in the air.

Figs showed off his Saint Bernard and played Frisbee with Bax.

Bax said he always wanted a dog.

Margo brought out lemonade. "Elliott, you want to give it a try like we talked about?"

"Yeah, Elliott," said Nory. "Do it!"

Elliott flicked his finger at the lemonade, icing it over. "Slushies for everyone!" he proclaimed.

There was a cheer.

A small, slight girl appeared from within the house.

"Pepper!" Nory cried. "You made it."

"Figs, turn back *now*," Margo commanded.

He immediately took her advice. Back in his human form, he cleared his throat and adjusted his shirt. If Pepper had scared him, even for half a second, he wasn't about to show it.

Pepper stood shyly at the edge of the yard. Nory dashed over, took her by the forearm, and dragged her toward the others. "Lemon slushies by Elliott," she said as she handed Pepper one.

Pepper smiled. "Yum."

Margo's cell phone buzzed. She frowned and fished it out of her pocket. "Hello?" She listened for a moment, and her eyes flew to Nory. "Actually, now isn't a good . . . well, all right . . ." She sighed and held the phone out to Nory. "It's for you."

Nory didn't understand. Her friends were right here, every last one of them. Who could be calling?

She stepped away from the group and raised the phone to her ear. "Hello?"

It was Dalia and Hawthorn, together.

"How did the test go?" Dalia asked.

"Did you pass?" Hawthorn asked.

"Are you done being upside-down?"

"Can you come home?"

Nory leaned against a tree. So much had happened that she didn't know where to begin. Also, her feelings were hurt. The test had been last week, and they were just calling her now.

"I failed," she said. "I have to stay in UDM."

"Oh, sweetie, I'm so sorry," Dalia exclaimed. "Maybe you can try again?"

"You have to," Hawthorn said. His tone reminded Nory of how bossy he could be. "You'll have to practice harder, that's all. Harder and longer and better."

"I do?"

"You're not going to give up, are you? Don't you want to come home?"

Nory wound a strand of her big hair around her finger. Of course she wanted to go home. She missed Hawthorn and Dalia and Father. She missed her room, her big house, and the pretty green lawns of her old hometown. She missed all sorts of things.

But here she had Aunt Margo, who liked her just the way she was. Aunt Margo got her library books, took her flying sometimes, and let her eat lunches of starch, grease, and sugar.

She had Figs, who did an awesome Saint Bernard, and Ms. Starr, who was never afraid to look silly and who believed in talking about feelings.

And the other kids in the UDM class. She had them, and they had her.

"I have to go," she said into the phone. "I have friends over."

"You do?" Hawthorn asked. "Upside-Down friends?"

"Yep," Nory said. "We're having slushies."

"Oh," Hawthorn said. He breathed in and out. "Well, don't forget to practice your black kitten."

"Bye," Nory said, and she pressed the button to end the call.

She lowered the phone to her side. Bax threw the Frisbee to Andres, who threw it to Pepper, who threw it to Elliott.

Elliott fumbled it and handed it to Willa, who threw it to Marigold, who threw it to Sebastian, who dropped it. Sebastian always dropped it.

"I can't help it!" he cried. "Its sound waves are so bright!"

Nory drank her slushie and watched her friends.

She wasn't sure she wanted to practice being normal anymore. She wasn't sure she wanted to go back home to Father.

Was that giving up?

Or was she just choosing something different?

Maybe, thought Elinor Boxwood Horace, *I like being upside-down.*

Nory, Bax, and friends return for another
upside-down adventure in:

UPSIDE★DOWN MAGIC #2: STICKS & STONES

Acknowledgments

An exploding box of thank-yous to:

Our Fluxers:
David Levithan, Kelly Ashton, Elizabeth Parisi, Ellie Berger, Lori Benton, Tracy van Straaten, Bess Braswell, Whitney Steller, Abby McAden, Aimee Friedman, Rachael Hicks, Lizette Serrano, Emily Heddleson, and everyone else at Scholastic.

Our Flickers:
Laura Dail, Barry Goldblatt, Elizabeth Kaplan, Tamar Rydzinski, Deb Shapiro, Arielle Datz, and Tricia Ready.

Our Flyers:

Robin Wassmerman, Courtney Sheinmel, Jennifer E. Smith, Elizabeth Eulberg, Bob, Gayle Forman, Maureen Johnson, Rose Brock, and Libba Bray.

Our Fuzzie-wuzzies:

Al, Jamie, Ivy, Maya, Mirabelle, Alisha, Hazel, Chloe, and Anabelle.

Our Flares:

Daniel, Randy, and Todd.

About the Authors

SARAH MLYNOWSKI is the author of many books for tweens, teens, and adults, including the *New York Times* bestselling Whatever After series, the Magic in Manhattan series, and *Gimme a Call*. She would like to be a Flicker so she could make the mess in her room invisible. Visit her online at www.sarahm.com.

LAUREN MYRACLE is the *New York Times* bestselling author of many books for young readers, including The Winnie Years (which begins with *Ten*), the Flower Power series (which begins with *Luv Ya Bunches*), and the Life of Ty series. She would like to be a Fuzzy so she could talk to unicorns and feed them berries. You can find Lauren online at www.laurenmyracle.com.

EMILY JENKINS is the author of many chapter books, including the Toys Trilogy (which begins with *Toys Go Out*) and the Invisible Inkling series. Her picture books include *Lemonade in Winter, Toys Meet Snow*, and *The Fun Book of Scary Stuff*. She would like to be a Flare and work as a pastry chef. Visit Emily at www.emilyjenkins.com.